The Deep Blue Crush

Mac Crow #3

By Clint Hollingsworth

Illustration by Clint Hollingsworth

Published by Icicle Ridge Graphics. For permission requests, write to the publisher, addressed "Attention: Permissions Coordinator," at the website address below.

www.clinthollingsworth.com
Printed in the United States of America

ISBN-13: 978-0-9975170-7-1

Cover design by Clint & Suzette Hollingsworth

Dedication

I put my wonderful wife Suzie in the dedication of my first book, along with a slew of other people. This one's all for her. Without Suzie, there would be no Mac Crow and not much of a Clint Hollingworth.

Thank you, my love. For everything.

CHAPTER ONE

I never thought I would die by fire.

It's strange, the things that go through your mind when a massive wall of flame is coming toward you, faster than most people can run. The little girl I was carrying wasn't so philosophical about it, she was just terrified.

I could hear her father crashing through the brush beside me, and I knew he was just as burdened carrying the small boy who was the girl's brother.

It didn't look like it was going to be a good day for any of us.

***

Our team, *Chambers and Associates Fugitive Retrieval Services*, had been enlisted by the county sheriff's department again this year when fire season broke out. Each year, we wound up spending a few weeks sitting at various barricades keeping people out of dangerous areas.

I climbed out of our SUV, stretching out the kinks, when Rosa slapped me across the belly. Her five foot nine should have been intimidated by my six foot two, but that was a forlorn hope. Nothing intimidated the lovely Ms. Fernandez, and certainly not the guy she was kissing on a regular basis. The other two members of our team pulled the stand-up barricades out of the back.

Vinnie Lugar and my Uncle Gil had met in the military, even though they were years apart in age. When they'd left the service, they'd decided to form a partnership in a company whose main purpose was to track down and re-jail people who skipped out on their bail bondsmen, er… bonds people. They'd recruited ex-marine Rosa to join them, when the business took off. I'd come along a few years later; family nepotism rather than military nepotism.

"Old timers in our area told me that the hottest part of the summer used to be two to three weeks in July," Vinnie said. "sometimes crossing into August. This year, we hit 100 degrees Fahrenheit by the last week of June. No wonder these fires break out and run." It was the second week of August now and reasonable temperatures had only been few and far between. The land had dried out accordingly.

"Hotter than hell out here in the open," my uncle said. "Mac, did you make sure to bring that sunshade?"

"Oh heck yeah. I'll go set it up a little way back there, off the road." It didn't take long to get everything put together, with canvas chairs and a cooler under the portable awning. Once that was all taken care of, it was time to delegate duties.

"Rosa and I will stay here at the barricade," Uncle Gil said, in his gravelly voice. "You and Vinnie scour the campgrounds up the canyon and round up any campers still fool enough to be in this area. We'll stay here and keep any new fools from going up the road." My uncle, a tall, rangy man in his late fifties, had a face like chipped granite. Since he was our employer, we usually didn't question his directives.

But there are alway exceptions.

"Gil," Rosa said, "I could go with Mac, and you and Vinnie…"

"Nope. I need you here to intimidate anyone who thinks they know better than the Forest Service and the Chelan County Sheriff's Department. One look at your angry face, and they'll back right down."

"Like you need me," she replied. "One look at your stoney face, and all the bears in this area go frantically searching for a hole to crawl into."

"Are you saying I have resting grouch face?"

"I can attest to this, Uncle Gil," I said.

My uncle couldn't help but grin, but he said, "Mac and Vinn'll handle emptying the campgrounds. Rosa can help me get these barricades better placed. The fire might not ever make it into this valley, but I wouldn't bet the farm on that. And you know we'll be fending off tourists and newspaper reporters."

Normally, as much as I liked Vinnie, I'd have loved to have had Rosa along. She and I had become close while on a particularly harrowing tracking case during the winter. We'd been tracking a supposed murderer in the Pasayten Wilderness. The case hadn't remotely gone according to plan, and we were almost killed more than once.

"Sorry, lover boy," Vinnie said, climbing into our black 'War Wagon', the heavily reinforced SUV usually used to find fleeing felons. "Looks like you're stuck with me."

"Fate's cruel," I said, climbing into the passenger seat. Vinnie put it in gear and we left the pavement's end, heading up canyon.

Vinnie was a big man, and one of my best friends, a cheerful fellow whose six-foot-four could be intimidating as hell when a felon tried to argue with him. He was clean-shaven, as numerous attempts to grow out his scraggly brown beard had proven discouraging.

"How many campgrounds are up this road?" he asked, rolling his window up to avoid the dust flying from the unpaved lanes. I turned the AC back on.

"We've got no less than seven," I said, looking at the TOPO map I'd brought with us. "Plus about ten vacation cabins which, fortunately, are all in one area."

"Geez," Vinnie said, "no wonder the local cop shop is overextended. All these different roads, all these different campgrounds. They must need to have a team on every major forest service road in this area, and this fire is huge. I think it affects every access point into the national forest around here."

"Dry year. Seems like they get drier every season. Hopefully bystanders are smart enough to stay clear."

Vinnie drove the big SUV up the dusty road until we reached our first campground, and to our relief, it was completely empty. It took less than ten minutes to traverse the entire place and make sure that all the camp sites were vacant. People were evidently smarter than we gave them credit for, and didn't want to stay in an area that was possibly going to be on fire.

Within forty-five minutes we'd covered three more and were batting a thousand. No one was in the campgrounds until we reached the site at the magnificent waterfall that was the main attraction of the entire valley. A few stragglers, sitting at the campsites near the base of the falls had difficulty believing they wouldn't be safe from fire-related problems in that wet environment. We quickly disabused them of the notion.

"Jesus," one impressively-bearded young man whined, "here's the MAN, always gettin' in the common folks' face. Thank you, dickhead authority figures."

Vinnie and I, being far from the elite, had to swallow hot responses to remain professional.

"Dude," Vinnie said, "I just don't want you to get your face flamed off. Fire's burnin' super hot. Even these cedars down here are a danger, so please, just get packed and get outta here."

The idiot grumbled some sort of "I'm such a rebel" B.S., but started loading his car with the help of his girlfriend.

"If he's still here when we come back," I said, "rock, paper, scissors to see which of us gets to put a boot up his stupid ass."

"I dunno," my partner said, climbing into the SUV. "Sometimes you just wanna let Darwinism have its way with guys like that to clean up the gene pool. Mr. Fuzz-Face there is old enough to know better."

"Old enough to know better seems to come later and later these days," I said.

"Kind of lofty rhetoric coming from you, Old Man Crow." I had only just passed my twenty-fifth birthday. Vinnie grinned, and I knew it probably took stern discipline on his part to not to say more. "I can't imagine why anyone would want to be in this valley, right now," he said. "Look at all this smoke! You'd think we were coming into LA during smog season."

"Or Beijing." I replied, "Hey, there's that bunch of cabins we're supposed to check. Turn here."

It was a group of smallish-looking vacation cabins, all on a single road. The majority of the area this far up the canyon was forest service land, but this one pocket was privately owned and had been subdivided into a quiet little summer community.

It took us quite a bit longer than the campgrounds to check. It was necessary to get out of the vehicle at each place, and knock loudly. While Vinnie did that, I circled each cabin trying to get a look inside. People sometimes hid from anyone in authority during evacuations, figuring they were somehow immune to nature's wrath. Thankfully there were none of those here, and we found no one until we came to the last cabin.

At that driveway, we'd barely gotten out of the SUV before we knew we had trouble. A sixty-ish woman dressed in a wide brimmed hat, work shirt and jeans was waiting for us. The stressed out look on her face spoke volumes as she made her way toward us at a fast walk.

"Help!" she yelled as I climbed out. "I need help!"

"Ma'am, you need to vacate this area as fast as you can! This--"

"I know that, you young doofus! I'm stuck here, no car, no phone!"

"No cell service out here," I said. "I see the problem."

"And my good for nothing kids in California haven't even bothered to try and check on me."

"How do you know? There's no cell service." I didn't know

her kids, maybe they were good for nothing, but let's be fair.

"I can stay with my friend Lisa in Waterville, but she's in Las Vegas for the next three weeks." She continued as if I hadn't spoken. "I need a ride out. I'm all packed. You're elected."

I could have argued, but I could see she was right. "Where's your gear? Let's get it in the truck."

"I'm Melinda," she said as we carried duffels and suitcases to the War Wagon. "I'm… sorry I snapped at you young man."

"Call me Mac. The fellow carrying your suitcases is Vinnie."

"Nice ta meetcha," Vinnie said, nodding. "Could be under better circumstances, though."

"Amen to that," Melinda said. She gestured at the belongings we were carrying. "Good thing about minimalist living though, when you've got to move, you can do it in about three trips to the car. Assuming you have a car."

"Minimalist, hunh? You and Mac should talk," Vinnie said. "He lives in an old Air Stream down on the Columbia."

Melinda looked at me, querying eyebrow raised.

"Yeah," I said, loading a duffle into the SUV. "I try to keep my stuff pretty limited, though books are not so easy."

"The three boxes you see on the porch there? Boxes of books."

"Mac can carry those. They look heavy." Vinnie set his load in the back and I went for the boxes. Melinda evidently was not one to sacrifice the important things in life. I glanced inside. The house was, as I expected, not cluttered, and tastefully furnished in log cabin type furniture.

"Too bad we have to leave your furniture, but just the gear you had on the porch filled our rig up."

Melinda's expression grew pained. "I love this little place, and I hope it doesn't burn, but I rent. The furniture isn't mine, and I'm not responsible for saving it from natural disasters.

Me and Cat-cat are outta here."

It was only then we noticed the cat carrier containing a rather round-eyed short hair tabby. Vinnie groaned.

"He's my best friend," Melinda told him. "He sure can't stay here."

"My aching sinuses… Okay, if you're going with us, we've gotta clear a couple more campgrounds, Melinda," Vinnie said.

"Then let's not dawdle."

***

We continued up the canyon, with one more campground to check. I could see smoke rising over the ridge but had no idea how far the fire was from us. In this dry season, the smoke plume rose miles into the air.

As dry as it was, the canyon was beautiful with the plant life frantically expanding to get its yearly quota of growth in. A squirrel made Vinnie slow down, not understanding that the center of the road wasn't a good place to take a sight-seeing tour. Looking off through the pines and big leaf maples, I saw a doe with a new fawn. I prayed to the Creator they'd all be spared the destruction and death consuming so much of the forest.

The people of North Central Washington state were showing a great deal of wisdom because the last couple of campgrounds were empty. But there's always someone to screw up the curve.

We had just entered the farthest campground in the valley, which was arguably the one closest to this fire consuming a good fraction of a national forest, when we saw them. A large, shiny Ford pickup was sitting in front of a medium-sized travel trailer and a man and a woman were arguing furiously. I don't even think they noticed us when we got out of the War Wagon.

"Goddammit, Jeannie! It was your flippin' job to keep

an eye on the kids while I got us ready to go!" The man, dressed in shorts and a Seahawks tank top, yelled at the top of his lungs.

"I put them in the trailer! I told them not to come out, so I could help you pack all this crap! I turned my back for five seconds so I could pack the coolers and chairs in their bags."

"You should have made sure they knew not to wander off!"

"If you hadn't been yelling at them – and me – all morning, they probably wouldn't have been scared!"

"I didn't mean nothin' by it. Someone had to take charge!"

The woman was drawing breath to reply when Melinda, who had followed Vin and me, broke in with a voice whose volume belied her small stature.

"Both of you shut up! Who's at fault doesn't matter! Finding your kids is what's important here." A momentary silence prevailed.

"Do you have any idea where they might have gone? General direction?" I asked.

"No," the woman moaned, a horrified expression coming to her face that made me want to cringe. "One moment they were here, then I looked up and they were gone."

"How many? Ages?"

"Um.. Five and seven. Our little boy Michael is seven, and Jillian is five."

"Vin, I bet they've gone towards the river. Just got that gut feeling. Get these two ready to roll and I'll see if I can find tracks."

"You think you can find them, find where they went?" the mother asked.

"If anyone can find tracks, Mac's your guy," Vinnie said. "We'll get 'em ready. Use your radio to keep me apprised."

"I'm going too," the father said. "Those are my kids."

"All right. Melinda, can you help Vinnie and this lady…"

"My name is Jeannie."

"..And help Jeannie get ready to roll?"

"You betcha," Melinda said. "I was handling travel trailers before you were born."

"Great. Okay.. Um…"

"Tom." the father said.

"Okay. Tom and I are going looking."

"Lot more smoke in the valley now," Vinnie said. "Hopefully the fire's not down in this drainage and it's just the wind, but be ready to book on outta here."

I nodded and Tom and I headed for the river.

"You think we can find them?" Tom asked. He looked like a typical working guy, with close-cropped UFC style hair, a boatload of unrelated tattoos and a few too many waffles under his belt. But the fear in his eyes told me that he loved his kids. "You a tracker or something?"

"Been tracking since I was ten years old."

"Oh God, I hope we can find their tracks."

"I think the odds are good," I replied as we arrived at the riverbank. I pointed at two petite sets of footprints. Fresh footprints.

"Michael! Jilly!" He yelled. No answer. The sound from the river wouldn't have allowed a reply to get far.

"They're heading downstream. Let's go." I started following the children's trail and it took me a few minutes to figure out what they were doing. The tracks would be facing the river one moment, then racing madly downstream the next.

What are they doing?

I could see holes where small river rocks had been pulled up and after a short time, I got it. They were chasing something, a stick most likely, that they had tossed into the river. They were following it, trying to nail it with rocks, pretty much like every child who had ever had a river with some rocks on the shore.

These kids had covered a lot of ground quickly. Now that I had a good inkling of what was going on, I didn't need to look for every single track, and began to trot downstream. This backfired on me shortly thereafter, as I realized there were no more tracks in front of me. My troubles were compounded by the smoke and the fact that kids are unpredictable. I coughed, the haze getting thicker by the moment. Not a good sign.

"Michael! Jilly!" Tom yelled. We didn't hear anything but the sound of the river.

After a short backtrack, I saw the barest imprint in a bit of dry moss. A few more feet and I saw more moss had been knocked off a log, then another track. From the size of the print, it was the little girl, and she was heading inland, back toward the general direction of the road. Seeing her footprint led me to her brother's, and their father and I began following their trail again.

"You hear that?" Tom asked, his expression perplexed.

I thought for a moment that he'd heard the kids, but then I heard it.

A roaring sound, a lot like someone had just breached a massive dam, or maybe a windstorm whipping down through the treed valley.

Then it clicked. Not a windstorm, a firestorm. The forest fires had crested the ridge, and they were moving down the hillside in front of us. I stumbled forward, trying to see the track through the haze.

"Tom, keep yelling for the kids, and don't stop. Make it loud as you can."

We moved forward, across mossy ground so dry it crunched under my feet. The plus side of that was the children's tracks stood out every time we hit an open area, and we were able to move faster. They were heading in the general direction of the road so they couldn't be too far ahead.

"Mac!" My radio blared out Vinnie's voice. "Come in. Fire is down the mountain, and we are cut off at the campground. Get to the river, NOW! It's coming your way!"

"Copy. What are you gonna do?"

"We're taking the War Wagon for a swim, but you got no

time to talk! The wind is sending the fire in your direction, man, and it's comin' quick!"

Just then, between Tom's yells for his children, I heard a high-pitched response. Tom and I both ran forward, and as we entered a small clearing, two small children, both obviously frightened, ran toward us.

"Daddy! We got lost!" the boy yelled.

"It's so smoky, Daddy," the little girl said, in her helium pitched voice. "It makes me cough."

Tom kneeled, hugging both at once, and started to give them a lecture on wandering away. I cut him off.

"No time for that! Pick up Michael, and I'll carry Jilly. That fire is coming our way, and we really are gonna want to be in that river ASAP."

As if to punctuate my words, a large boom came from the area of the campground.

"Wh-what the hell was that?" Tom said, picking up his son. I snatched up the little girl and began to trot towards the river.

"It could have been a big pine topping out. Vinnie said he was driving our SUV into the river to try to avoid the fire. That might've been your pickup. And if we don't get to that water right now, it could be us!"

"Shit!"

We began to run. I don't think the forty extra pounds we were each carrying slowed us down a bit: the fear of fire was a powerful adrenalin rush. Thank God for the engineering of the human body. Looking over my shoulder, I could see flecks of orange through the trees. I started to feel heat on my cheek.

"It's here! Go! Go! Go!"

We did the closest thing to a sprint we could manage with small children in our arms. Glancing to the left, I could see a pair of mule deer rushing alongside us. Small animals were sprinting all around us, and some just weren't going to make it, but this was every creature for himself. I started to feel heat on my back and Jilly pushed her face into my shoulder. Over the approaching roar, I could hear her high-pitched wails of fear.

Tom snagged a shoe on a protruding stick, not going down, but getting his weight well forward of his feet. He started to stumble. I reached for him, grabbing his collar, and pulled him back to vertical before he could go down.

"Stay up, stay up! For God's sake, don't fall!"

"I can see the river," he yelled. "Hundred yards!"

I felt an impact on my side, and was knocked off balance. I looked up to see the culprit, a yearling black bear that had barely noticed the collision as he ran past. I couldn't keep my feet, and went down in a three-point landing, trying not to crush the little girl. Tom stopped and turned toward me.

"Keep running!" I screamed, as I struggled back to my feet. "I'm right behind you!"

I covered Jilly's head with my hand as I began to run again, feeling the skin of the back of my neck start to cook.

I never thought I would die by fire. For the first time I wondered if I might lose this race. I thought of Rosa, my mom—and this little girl I carried.

Tom was just ahead, crashing through the brush, trying to ignore sharp limbs and edges, and seconds later we were out of the forest and moving as quickly as we could over the rocky bed of the depleted river. There was water, but it was only a few feet deep in most places. The entire north side of the river was turning into an inferno behind us.

"That way! The water's collected in a pool." I said, pointing downstream. A section of the river, probably fifteen feet deep in the spring, but now no more than eight, beckoned as the only place that offered safety. The heat rising from the approaching fire felt like it could broil us, even if we weren't directly in it.

"Can't we just keep going?" Tom yelled, pointing at the opposite bank. As he said it, a drifting storm of sparks landed on that side and flames began burning in only a few seconds.

More sparks were doing the same, and several fires broke out.

"Water's our best bet. That side's going to flare up quick with all those small fires, and then we'll be even worse off. Nowhere to run to."

"Whoa!" Tom said, as a big pine exploded on the bank we had come from.

We made our way over the round-rock riverbed and waded into the section of deeper water. It was about thirty yards in length before the river went shallow again. I hoped it would be enough. The heat rising from the shore was getting unbearable, and both children were crying. My pant legs, now wet, were steaming.

Finally we were in the water up to our necks when I realized we weren't alone. A few feet away, the young black bear watched me with dog-like eyes. He looked at me, I looked at him.

We both broke eye contact, not wanting trouble.

"Hold your nose a moment, honey," I told Jilly. She nodded and I dunked us both underwater for ten seconds. When we surfaced, I could feel the water on my face start to dry immediately.

Tom and Michael were also periodically dipping below the water too, trying to take away some of the blazing heat. A doe bumped me on my right side, and I saw several animals seeking shelter in the span of deeper water. Squirrels clung to logs and rock, half in and half out of the water. I didn't want to think about all the animals who hadn't made it to the river. It made my heart sick.

"I think it's starting to burn out," Tom said. He pointed to the bank of the river we had come from and I saw the flames were getting smaller as they ran out of fuel. Some of the trees were still burning but the fire was definitely falling off there. On the other side, the blaze had taken off up the hillside, leaving streaks of green untouched, interspersed between burnt sections.

The young bear waddled out of the water and headed for one of the green strips and so did the deer. Tom and I dragged ourselves from the river and upon one of the larger rocks on the bank. We quietly sat, listening to the roar of the fire as it receded, watching the animals as they left the rocky pool. All of us were coughing, and all of us were coming down off the adrenaline high.

"Daddy?" Michael asked his father, "is Mommy okay?"

"We'll go find her in a few minutes, son. We just need to get our breaths."

Tom looked over at me, worry in his eyes.

"I'm sure they're okay," I said.

Truth be told, I wasn't that sure.

CHAPTER TWO

***

Tom and I had trudged back to the campground, apprehensive of what we might find. Though the distance wasn't far, it was an unpleasant walk. The beautiful forest was now a scorched area of burnt trees and ash for soil, with some of the brushy areas still burning. The moss I had tracked the kids in was now gray powder and every few feet we found the scorched corpses of woodland creatures that hadn't been lucky or fast enough to reach the river.

It made me feel a great depth of sadness, though I knew these fires had been happening longer than people had been on the continent. We marched up the bed of the river, the banks still hot enough to melt the soles of our shoes.

I've spent a lot of my life training to be aware in nature, and it's truly gratifying being able to move among the wild places as a part of those places, not just as an alien passing through. But to every yin there is a yang. My heightened awareness also brings heightened sensitivity to what's around me.

What was around me now was pretty awful, even if it was a part of the natural world.

When we reached the campground, we were rewarded with the sight of all our people standing around the steaming SUV in a four-foot-deep stretch of the river.

We had just called out to them when Tom's wife ran to us, beginning a marathon display of affection to her babies.

"Dude," Vinnie said as I trudged up, relinquishing Jilly to her mom. "You are a sooty sight to see. Glad you made it. You okay? I couldn't raise you on your radio."

"We all tucked into a deep pocket of water downriver. I guess my 'talky' objected to being submerged."

Vinnie laughed. "We have GOT to find you a waterproof comm." It wasn't the first time that wet electronics had proven inconvenient for me.

"Me, Tom and the kids had a bit of a scare, but we made it okay. How's everyone here?"

"We all got in the wagon and put it out here. Got a bit warm, as you can tell by its paint job, but no one's really worse for wear, except maybe Jeannie's nerves. She was about out of her head worrying about those kids. And her husband, I guess."

"The river widens out here, so we didn't get cooked. Can't say much for their trailer and truck though," Melinda said, ashes caught in her gray hair. She pointed back along where our SUV's tire tracks led into the river and I saw that most of the campground had been consumed. In site number six, Tom's truck, trailer and most of the possessions they'd brought were black and melted-looking. The truck was still burning.

"Lets get the hell out of here," Jeannie said.

It was a quiet group of people seated in the now piebald War Wagon. Jeannie hugged her son one moment, then switched to her daughter, kissing each on cheeks and foreheads.

We drove back along the highway, Michael complaining that their mom was hugging them to death. I noticed Jilly didn't seem to mind at all.

I also noted that Jeannie, once she'd seen he was all right, had shyly stretched out her hand to Tom. She was well aware how close things had gotten, for her husband as well as her children.

Tom had confessed to me that his wife had wanted to leave yesterday, but he'd assured her the fire was too far away to be a problem for their favorite campout. He wasn't a bad guy. I was glad they were making peace offerings.

I was also glad we were all in one piece, vehicles notwithstanding.

We drove past the turn-off for the cabins, and Melinda looked wistfully in that direction. Fire had obviously come through here too.

"Can we do a quick check, Vinn?" I asked.

"I… okay, but I ain't stoppin'."

It was as bad as I'd imagined. Worse even. Only two of the cabins were untouched. The two that still stood were those whose owners had the foresight to clear the pines out to a hundred yards from the structures. They were like islands in a sea of black.

Melinda's cabin was still burning.

"Well, I guess that's that. It was a nice place to live, but looks like Cat-cat and I are done here."

***

We pulled up to the check point, and Uncle Gil approached the driver's window, motioning for Vinnie to roll it down. Rosa was walking up on my side and I rolled the passenger window down also.

"What the hell happened up there?" Uncle Gil said, obviously trying to keep his cool. "We lost contact after you checked in at those canyons." He looked at the state of the SUV, and the furrow between his brows grew even deeper.

"Canyon gets narrow up there toward the last camp-grounds," Vinnie told him. "Narrow and rocky. Can't bounce a radio or a cell signal out. We found some folks who hadn't got the word…"

"I got the word!" Melinda piped in from where she sat between us, Cat-cat in her lap. "Just couldn't get a ride out till these two knights rescued me."

"Us too," Jeannie said. "They rescued us too."

"Yeah. There were a pair of lost kids, Gil," Vinnie told him. "That took some time to get them. It was close. Your nephew's tracking magic saved the day."

Uncle Gil turned and glared at the parents, who had the good sense not to say anything.

Gilbert Chambers was very quick to assess the situation as per usual. We were generally in the business of either rescuing or pursuing the stupid and careless, so I might have thought he'd be used to it.

Nope.

He seemed more unhappy about the damage to the truck than about the possible damage to his crew. I knew he was a lot more concerned than he appeared though. Still, I wasn't about to tell him about my ruined radio.

Yet.

Rosa looked in at me, an expression on her face I'd never seen before. "Mac, you okay?"

"I'm fine, just a little singed. We're…" she cut me off, grabbing my face and pressing her forehead against mine.

"We were so worried!" she said, unable to keep the usual stoic expression she wore under stress.

"It's okay, we're okay. It all worked out."

"Please, just promise me that someday you'll try not to use your damn superpower."

"I'll try." I laughed. My superpower, we always joked, was the amazing ability to get into trouble.

"Hey Gil," Vinnie said. "these folks need a ride into town. And Mac and I both could use showers to get this soot off. Can you and Rosa do without us for a while?"

"Yeah. Go get cleaned up. We're supposed to be off here at nine P.M. Come back and get us then."

"Yeah. Gotta keep out the looky-loos," Rosa said with a sour tone.

"Okay. See you at nine." My uncle stepped away from the truck, and I waved at Rosa as Vinn pulled away. I looked back in the rearview mirror as they stood by the barricade. We'd set up in a section of road that wasn't treed but had green grass from a nearby farmer's irrigation. The chance that the fire could get to them was extremely low, but I wished we were bringing them with us.

It was a quiet drive down the valley toward the Columbia River. Two miles later, we were taken aback to see a section of hillside burning ahead of us. It was moving toward the road much more slowly than our earlier wind-driven experience, but that could change rapidly with just a breeze. Here, the grass was not irrigated, and was crunchy dry. The fire was slowly working its way down to a stand of trees near the road.

Vinnie sped up. Not a good place to dawdle.

"So, Tom, Jeannie," I said, "you live in Wenatchee? We can drop you off."

"Holy crap!" Vinnie exclaimed. I had been scratching the cat under his chin, attempting to calm it, when our driver's tone made me look up. My own mouth dropped open.

We were playing chicken with an airliner, a two-engine jet that looked like it should be the shuttle from New York to Chicago. It was flying up the narrow valley, below the ridgeline. As airliners go it was pretty small, but it seemed to fill most of the valley in front of us.

"Mommy! Look!" I heard Michael chirp out. "Is it going to hit us?"

The jet suddenly rolled a bit to one side, effortlessly skimming the north side of the valley. As it approached the fire on the hill, I saw a red cascade fall from its belly, enveloping the fire. The jet arced upward, cleared the hills, and flew off again toward the southeast. The fire on the ridge was noticeably smaller now.

A fine red mist of fire retardant covered our windshield, and Vinnie kicked in the squirters and the wipers. He and I looked at each other and we both said the only word that would apply.

"Awesome!"

"Glad I don't have to wash this rig," Melinda said.

***

It was around nine o'clock later that night when we rolled up to the barricade to pick up Uncle Gil and Rosa. The fire had moved out of the valley, making large black swaths on the hillsides, and we could see an ominous orange glow from the next watershed over. Even with the retardant bombers, it looked like the fire would reach the Columbia River by morning. If that happened it would either stop at the wide lake formed behind Rocky Reach Dam, or it would head upriver, which was the way with more fuel.

Rosa came up to the SUV, doing a last check on the barricade we were leaving, carrying her gear and a small cooler. As she tossed her things in the back storage area, I saw her look at the paint on the rear of the War Wagon that had stripped off when we ran it through the car wash.

"What did you guys do to this vehicle?" she said as she walked up to me.

"We did our best to not let it become a four-wheeled firebomb," Vinnie told her, exasperation in his voice. "Who knows, if it hadn't had all that armoring and reinforcing, we might've had to leave it in the middle of the river, burning like that Tom guy's truck."

"Whoa, Vinn," she said. "Wasn't criticizing, just commenting on the old girl's sad state."

"New paint job," Uncle Gil said, throwing his own gear in the back, "and she'll be right as rain, though that left rear tire looks a little dicey." He walked up to get in the driver's seat and noticed that Melinda and Cat-cat were sitting in the same spot they'd been in earlier.

"Er… Hello?" he said.

"Uncle Gil, Melinda needs our help and…" I started.

"She's in hard straights with this fire," Vinnie interjected.

"Boys!" Melinda cut us off. "If I'm going to ask someone

for help, I'd best do it myself, face to face." She exited the SUV. I had to give her props. My uncle is as tall as Vinnie, and the years have given him a craggy Clint Eastwood-ish face that looks like the definition of intimidating.

He looked at me, then at Vinnie, one eyebrow raised. He then looked down at Melinda, who stood about half his height. She looked him straight in the eyes without flinching.

"Awright, let's hear it," he said.

"Well," she said, swallowing hard. "I just made Social Security four months ago, and I retired. I've been living out here, and trying to hardly spend anything, because my retirement savings isn't enough to live on."

"So you don't have anything other than social security, Ma'am?" he asked. Gilbert was a self-made man who generally thought people had no one to blame but themselves for the mess they were in, but it was often his business to help those same people. His professionalism generally took over when he needed to delve deeper.

She must have sensed his underlying slight because she grew defensive. "I had a good retirement! I saved very carefully. I'd bet that at one time I had a better retirement savings set aside than anyone standing here," she said with indignation. "I made the terrible mistake of trusting someone to help me manage that money. He 'Madoffed' me."

"You're saying an investment broker put you in this situation?"

"That's right. Well, he said he was an investment broker."

"There are laws against that, you know."

"Even if they catch him, I'm not getting my money back. Plenty of brokers lose their clients' money without any repercussions whatsoever. But now I know my 'broker' wasn't a real one. He was a con man."

"Is that what happened?"

"I guess I was stupid. He was actually involved in illegal

activities. But my money is still gone."

"You can go after him for criminal activity. Have you filed a claim with the Securities and Exchange Commission?"

"You bet I have."

"No luck?"

"Nope. No one can even find him, now. If they did, it could take years—and by then the money will all be spent."

"Hmmm. . ." Uncle Gil seemed deep in thought and I knew the wheels were turning.

"And what about your home?" he asked. "Don't you have home insurance?"

"That cabin was a rental – the landlord was a friend who gave me a great deal. Now I've got to somehow live on $700 a month. I just paid my rent and bought my paltry groceries, and now I have no place to live, no groceries and twenty-eight days until my next pitifully small allowance from Social Security. Right now, I don't even have a car for Cat-cat and I to live in."

Uncle Gil looked at Vinnie and me again.

"I thought you had kids?" Vinnie asked. "Why can't they send you a couple a hundred a month?"

I could see from her expression that Melinda had asked herself that same question, but she replied cooly, "They live in California. It's very expensive. You'd be surprised how much it costs to maintain a pool."

Maybe her kids are good-for-nothing.

"Uh, Gil…" Vinnie said, "Mac and I sorta mentioned how you got that big ol' six-bedroom farmhouse…"

"And how you've kinda taken in Ol' Ed," I said "and we thought that…"

"You thought it was my job to do something about this lady… what was your name again?"

"Melinda," she said. "It's only for a few weeks until my friend comes back from Vegas."

"You have a lot of friends for someone who is asking for my help."

She returned Gilbert's glare. "I'm not asking for charity, you know. I can clean and cook. I'll earn my rent. Believe me, I wouldn't ask for help except Cat-cat doesn't like motels—no kitchen and they run $300 per week for a dump. You know—"

Gil appeared personally interested for the first time. "Wait. Cook? What can you cook?"

She shrugged. "The usual. Nothing fancy. Fried chicken, mashed potatoes, biscuits and gravy, spaghetti, roast beef, pancakes, omelets, pork chops and apples—"

"Fried chicken?" he demanded. "Is it good?"

"The best you've ever had." Melinda said, realizing which way the wind was blowing.

"And biscuits?"

"And corn-on-the-cob and green beans and ham hocks if you want them," she said, with a slightly nonchalant aire. "Oh, and I bake pretty well too."

Gil's expression took on the rare countenance of charitable kindness. One I'd seen only a few times in my life. "It seems to me Old Ed is getting skinny. I don't care about myself, but he's served his country and he needs to be fed."

"A man needs to eat." I tended to see both sides of a story, but this subject only had one perspective as far as I was concerned.

Uncle Gil turned to the lady present. "Listen here, Ma'am, I already got rid of one woman who was a pain in my ass, and I'm not putting up with any interference. The minute you cause me any trouble, and don't live up to your side of the bargain, you're out. I'm not running a free boarding house."

"I'll earn my keep, Mister Chambers," she replied. "And my name is Melinda."

"Melinda. All right, here's how this is going down. I can

see from where I stand that this cat here," his gaze, now on Melinda's tabby, softened a little, "needs help. Since he owns you, I guess I'd be heartless to make him leave you at the pound, Melinda, so it looks like I'll have to let him bring you along."

"Oh dear God, thank you!"

"This is of course, contingent on whether or not *my* owner, one Mr. McGow, has any major objections," he said with a slight smile. Looking up, Uncle Gil noticed the looks on his team's faces. "Quit grinning you buncha idiots. Now let's go. I desperately need a shower."

We all climbed into the SUV, perhaps breathing a quiet sigh of relief. As I sat, I looked back toward the mountains. I couldn't help but hope this fire didn't harm anyone else. The glow showing over a nearby ridge didn't reassure me.

CHAPTER THREE

***

The day after, we had the first rain in two months. It was a light shower, lasting maybe an hour and a half, but at my little home along the Columbia River, you could feel the plants almost sigh with relief. The fire had calmed a bit in our area, though it was still burning relentlessly farther north. Our team had been out on various road block duties for almost two weeks and it was good to finally have a few days off.

I was walking up the rocky lava rock road that led down to my Airstream trailer. My little plot of land was grandfathered into a section of the Colockum Wildlife Refuge, and it was my little slice of heaven. It sat near the base of a basalt cliff, and a small year-round stream turned my land into an oasis in the sagebrush desert. The trailer wasn't large, but when you lived in a spot like this, extra stuff just weighed you down. As I was buying the land from my mom, that was just as well, since most of my money went to my mortgage.

For fire safety, I had promised my mom I would help her clear the brush that was working its way closer to her ranch-style home and barn. As I passed the gate to my part of our shared property and hit the flat, I took a deep breath.

Nothing like the smell of sagebrush after a rainfall.

Once on the dirt road that separated our respective houses, I noted all the various animal tracks, now shown in brilliant clarity against the rain-pocked dirt. Coyote, pheasant, quail all had been there earlier, their tracks appearing smooth compared to the rain-flecked dirt. There was something on the road ahead of me. As I got closer, it looked like a clump of feathers.

"Well, howdy."

The Swainson's hawk sitting in the middle of the road noshing on a small rabbit looked at me with vague irritation. She promptly picked up her prey and flew thirty yards away, straight down the road, of course. I would have just avoided her by going around through the bunch grass and sagebrush, but everything was dripping after the rain, and I was wearing a cotton work shirt and jeans.

"Y'know, if you'd just fly to the left or right," I said, coming up on her again, "we could avoid all this. I could just use the road and you'd be left in peace to eat your meal." This very reasonable suggestion was lost on my raptor friend as she flew another thirty yards down the road, carrying her prey.

I rubbed the bridge of my nose, and then circled a good fifty yards around her.

"You look wet," my mom said, as I walked up her driveway.

"Just damp. Gonna probably get wet and muddy anyway, pulling out those two big sagebrush clumps you want removed."

"I hate pulling them out, but they're so close to the barn," she said. "If it would just stay reasonably cool like today I wouldn't worry, but the way this summer has gone, I'm constantly afraid of a brush fire coming down the hill and catching it on fire."

I took the brush hook, a small machete, a shovel, pry bar and a saw to where I was to start working. It sounds like an arsenal, but two of these sagebrush plants were large ones, and I knew getting them out would be a huge chore. After fooling around with trying to pry them up by the roots, I got serious, lying on a small tarp in the dirt, and starting sawing through the wrist thick trunks.

"How's Rosa?" Mom asked, handing me a small bit of

heaven in the form of a cold beer. “Haven’t seen her for a few days.”

“She’s good. She went to visit her girlfriend in the Tri-Cities.”

“Seems that you two are getting pretty serious.”

I sure hope so. “She seems to like me, for some strange reason.”

“No accounting for taste,” Mom said, smiling. “I’m just trying to get a feel for how things are going.”

Danger! Danger! My spidey sense began to tingle.

“Ohhh? Why?”

“Just trying to calculate how long it will be before I have a grandchild to play with. I’m thinking a little girl, but a boy would…”

The world went silent, the only sound was the breeze through the tall grasses. Then, of course, raucous laughter.

“Oh Mac! Ha ha ha! If only I had a mirror so I could show you the look on your face.” she said, gulping air between explosions of mirth. “If there was a picture in the dictionary for the term ‘deer in the headlights’, your photo would be at the top of the listing.”

“Mom! Fer Pete’s sake, Rosa and I’ve only been together five or six months!”

“Oh, my day is made.”

“Yeah. Hilarious. You should take that on the road.”

I was dragging the sawed-off fronds to a slowly growing brush pile in the field behind the barn when my phone rang with a particularly obnoxious red-alert sound.

“Hey, Uncle Gil. What’s up?”

“MacKenzie? I need for you to meet us at the office. How soon can you get there?”

“I’m up at mom’s, covered in grime. Take me about an hour to walk home, get showered and drive in.”

“Get there ASAP. We may have a lead on this guy that

screwed over Melinda, and best of all, he has a bounty on his head."

"I'll be there in forty-five."

Mom watched me talk to Uncle Gil with curiosity on her face. "A new job?"

"We.. Uh… kinda picked up a stray." I told her about Melinda and her tale of woe. As I narrated the story of how she'd been swindled, a strange look came over my mom's face, like a combination of apprehension and embarrassment.

"Mom? What's up?"

"It's nothing," she said, turning toward the ranch house. "You'd better get a move on, or you'll be late."

***

I was dry and clean as I pulled up to our unobtrusive little office behind Visconti's Italian restaurant. We keep a fairly low profile, for security reasons. The sign for our business is in our window, and measures about eleven inches wide.

I saw Uncle Gil's Explorer parked in the lot, covered in its usual patina of dust. Walking in the door, I saw my uncle, Melinda and, to my surprise Ed Burnbaum, my wilderness mentor and now permanent caretaker at Uncle Gil's ranch.

"Hey, Ed. Decide to come into the big city?"

"Wenatchee. Oh yeah, there's a big city for ya." He glanced at Melinda. "I…uh just came in for moral support." If I wasn't mistaken, he blushed slightly. Of course, I must've been mistaken, the tough old Viet Nam vet never was one to blush.

"Mac," Uncle Gil called me over, pointing at the screen of his laptop, "take a look at this."

I looked over his shoulder into the face of a the blondest man I had ever seen. His hair, mustache and brows were almost white, and it was a little disconcerting on someone who was obviously still youngish.

"Meet Jordan Johnson, a.k.a. Jim Johnson, a.k.a. Davis Fallon," Uncle Gil said. "He has bilked many more people out of their nest-eggs and rainy day funds than Melinda here.

Many more. He has warrants out for his arrest in six states, and there is a sizable reward for his arrest. There is an even more sizable reward offered by a conglomeration of people he's swindled that have banded together to find this jack-hole."

"I like finding and busting jack-holes, Uncle Gil."

"We both do," he said. "And when doing that makes us able to pay our bills, I like it even more. That's why I'm going to employ your Internet tracking skills to try and skip-trace the S.O.B. Melinda, I need for you to tell Mac what you told Ed and I about this guy. Who knows? Maybe we can get back some of that cash for you."

"Does anyone know if this 'conglomeration' has put investigators on this?" I asked.

My uncle started to say something, but Melinda was out of her chair, face reddening, interrupting him.

"Oh hell yes, they did! They spent $10,000 on those losers they hired, only to receive a thirty-page report along with a huge bill that essentially said 'We can't find the guy' and that was that!" Had it been possible for steam to emerge from human ears, Melinda would have fogged up the room. "I paid my part, then told the group I was out. I wasn't the only one. Good money after bad."

"Did you receive a copy of the report? And do you still have it?" I asked.

"Hell yes! That's how I knew the investigators were crap. I have it all in a file folder along with all the correspondence I got from this bastard Jordan Johnson."

"Good. I'll need copies of it all, so that I don't wind up spending a lot of time covering the same ground."

"Way ahead of you." Melinda reached into her lime green daypack and handed me a thick folder. "I almost threw this away in disgust and despair. Really glad I hung onto it, now."

"Me too." I glanced through the contents. It was a dense pile of paperwork.

"It's going to take me a while just to look through and

process all this. I'm probably gonna need some help from Rosa." I turned to my uncle. "Since you were good enough to pay for my internet connection out at the trailer, I think I'll take it all home with me and read through it there."

"We'll make this your side project when we don't have any active business," he said. "When we're not stalking a bail jumper, I want you to spend at least a couple of hours a day following up on this."

"Hmmmm. And do I get to charge you for research time?" I asked, knowing the best place to needle my uncle was in his checkbook. "I mean research from any other source costs..."

"That's why I have you on staff, Skippy. You get your cut if anything comes from it, as you well know."

"Can't blame a guy for trying."

"Like the initiative," he said, much to my surprise. "Good for young people to learn to negotiate, but we'll do things like we always have."

"Yes, boss."

If the truth be told, I was elated just to be on staff. Most parents help their kids get jobs, but my mom was not one of those. I was all she had since my dad died. She had expressly *not* wanted me to work for Uncle Gil, and she still didn't. This, originally, had given him a huge disincentive to give me anything except the desk jobs.

Nope. Not what I was cut out for.

A bounty-hunting business needs a tracker, even if he's following digital footprints, but it also needs people who can get the hard jobs done in the field. It had taken me some time to convince Gilbert that I could be trusted to stay alive – it was in my best interest, after all--and that I had the right to risk my life every day just as he did. I'd proven that, even with a lot of resistance from my family.

I can't say why I loved the job--I was originally trained solely as a wilderness tracker--but turns out, hunting bad guys was in my blood.

CHAPTER FOUR

***

That evening, I sat on my deck, wading through the mass of paperwork Melinda had handed me. It was not the thrill-a-minute job one might think.

I had separated the information into two piles: The first was documents that she had received from Johnson, giving her false information about her money. The second contained all the information she had been given by the group of victims and their investigators.

The papers from the scammer were very well done, looking like one might see from a legitimate brokerage house. Charts showed her money had started working for her and gained an astounding 18 percent interest from almost day one. There was even a booklet that looked like a very convincing annual report. Melinda had invested almost everything she had, $375,000. Within a month she started receiving dividend payments of $2,100 per month.

It was a case of being trapped by one's own optimism. Having talked with Mel a bit at the office, I found that she'd been a bookkeeper most of her life, working for a company that had partially matched her 401(k) deposits. She'd been smart enough to save as much as possible, but when her swindler had offered her a steady retirement income through dividends, without having to use her savings, she'd jumped at the chance. While I was sure there were brokers who could've indeed made this happen, I doubted many of them would guarantee 18 percent profit as Johnson had.

The portfolios weren't made up of publicly traded stocks, but were in fact some sort of revenue-producing bond funds. Websites for each of the major funds, were channeled through Johnson's business website. I went in to my laptop to see what I could learn about each, but every page-link that Melinda had been given came up *domain for sale*.

The dividend had been paid directly to her for eight months, supposedly without touching her invested money, an interest payout.

After the eighth month however, no payment came.

A sound made me look up from the paperwork, and I saw Rosa's RAV coming down the switchback basalt-based road to my trailer.

I'd be lying if I didn't admit seeing her filled me with happiness. Rosa was a beautiful woman, but it was the whole package that had me by the heart. She was tough, smart and could be quite dryly funny when the notion took her. She also had a strong sense, a need you might say, for justice. We had that in common.

One look at her stormy face when she got out of her car, however, made me think the trip to the Tri-Cities hadn't gone according to plan.

"Hey there gorgeous," I said, "*¿que pasa?*"

"Glad to be back here," she said, kissing me. "I missed you."

"How was the Tri-Cities?"

"I love Graciella, but honestly, that girl makes some of the stupidest decisions man-wise of anyone I know."

"Oh boy, I take it you met the new boyfriend, and he didn't measure up."

"Oh, he's a charmer, actually. Kind of a cross between Sylvester Stallone and a gorilla. But he's only charming until he realizes you're not buying his act."

"It was that bad?"

"In this case. Mac, my mother used to drag home guys like this occasionally, super nice at first, but if you paid attention, there was just that subtle hint of an edge. Everything would be all wine and roses at first, then little freedoms would disappear. Six months later, none of us could leave the house without 'the boyfriend's' permission." She stared off into the distant past for a moment, hand unconsciously running though her hair. "A guy like this was what finally put me on the streets at fifteen."

"A hidden creep, then?"

That's a good way to put it. My mom's most heinous boyfriend came to us when I was fourteen. At first it was taking over our lives, but as I started to… mature… he kept getting close to me. Always bumping into me, hand or arm brushing my chest. When he started standing in my doorway, just looking at me and not saying anything, I could see where it was going, and I left."

"That's just…"

"Yeah. I had to go back when I was sixteen and drag my brother and little sister out of there to live with my aunt, but she couldn't possible support all three of us and her own brood. I wound up living with a girl gang 'til I was eighteen and went into the marines."

We were quiet a moment, looking out over the Columbia River. I wished in situations like this, I was better at knowing what to say. Instead of something comforting, I dodged and said, "So, what do you want to do about Graciella's problem?"

"Got nothing concrete. Since my laptop is at my apartment, I'd like to get on yours and do a background check."

"Uncle Gil pays for our subscriptions to all these sites, we might as well get his money's worth." I said, "Got to do a little background checking myself. I'm hoping you can help me."

"Oh?"

I explained our discussion with Melinda and subsequent decision to see what I could find out about Jori Johnson.

"Wow. Gotta give that ol' gal credit. She's got Gil wrapped around her little finger," Rosa said. "Normally you can't get him to move on anything without a great chance of cash landing in our laps. This sounds like it's gonna be a hard one to sort."

"Oh ye of little faith."

"Not dissin' your online tracking skills, baby. But guys like this make a profession out of shining people on, getting their money then disappearing completely. I'd guess this Johnson guy is pretty good at it if he has this many people tryin' to find him."

"Won't know 'til I try. Both of us on this together, and I bet we can find him."

"Happy to join the cause," she said. "But first, I came right here and didn't stop off at the apartment, and I really could use a shower."

"I see," I said, with a nonchalant air. "Do you… need any help with that?"

She smiled at me, looking through long lashes as dark as night. "I might. You better come in there with me, just to make sure."

"I always try to be helpful."

"Yes, you do."

***

The shower took quite a bit longer than showers usually do. I sat out on the deck, the pleasant memory of smooth tanned skin under my fingers on my mind and contentment in my heart.

Rosa was on the laptop. One thing I had learned in our short time as a couple was to let her have space when she was working on a project. When in deep thought she tended to snap at me when I broke her concentration, and then she'd feel badly about it later. This cycle had caused some minor strife between us early on, until I finally got a clue and left her to her business when she needed me to.

At the moment, my own prey was taking a good amount of the run-time in my mind. There was no doubt Jori Johnson would be hard to track. But from what I could see of the report given to the victims by the private investigators, they had only done the standard checks. When that had turned up nothing concrete, they'd said the man couldn't be found, pocketed their well-padded fee, and that was that.

There had really been no…inspiration. No attempt at a "eureka" moment. When the trail had grown cold, they'd given up.

This was the difference between P.I.s and bounty hunters. We didn't get paid jack squat unless we produced. P.I.s put in their time, and sent out a bill, regardless of results.

P.I.s could also get away with things that bounty hunters legally could not. That's one of the reasons Uncle Gil had made sure his staff was licensed for both.

"Mr. Johnson," I said to the slowly appearing stars. "Wherefore art thou, shyster?"

The basalt cliffs behind my house had turned dark gray in the coming twilight, and the quarter moon peeked over the Earth's rim downriver. Stars began to appear in the gradient colors of the sky, and for a moment I was tempted to invoke the 'first star I see tonight' wish clause.

I wondered just how much Uncle Gil was willing to spend to let me research this. I really thought it might be good to interview a few of the other victims face to face, but I didn't look forward to trying to leverage expense money out if him to do so.

Rosa came out and sat in one of my beat up deck chairs. In the faint light from the lamp inside, her face was enigmatic, seeming both disturbed and excited.

"What?" I asked.

"Graciella's new boyfriend, David Martinelli, is indeed in our database." She said, *"Desgraciado."*

"Your instincts are good. How's it look?" If Rosa didn't like him, and the word she just said didn't sound like a compliment, I doubted it was going to be news her friend Graciella would appreciate.

"I'm not sure if this is better or worse, Mac. He has an outstanding bench warrant for his arrest."

I could see the dilemma; we could cause this man a great deal of difficulty, and probably make a profit doing it. But what would that do to Rosa's relationship with her gal pal? I decided not to offer an opinion.

"What's the warrant for?"

"Take a guess."

"Domestic violence?"

"Yep. And violating a restraining order, and failure to appear." She looked up at the silhouetted cliffs behind us. "As I said earlier, Graciella has a talent for finding the wrong men."

"So, do we point this out to Uncle Gil? Are you going to tell your friend?"

She sat there pensively, hand running though her hair again, not answering. I got up, went inside and got us both a beer. Opening hers, I set it next to her on the little metal and ceramic plant stand I used just for this purpose and sat down. I waited while she thought it out.

"I have to at least tell her," she said. Her tone was decisive, if not pleased.

"Think she'll listen?"

"Maybe a twenty-percent chance of that. More likely she'll get pissed off and tell me not to tell her what to do." She slumped in her deck chair and took a swig of beer. "There's no way she's gonna be happy on this thing."

"Not unless she has a moment of enlightenment and gets rid of the guy before he takes over her life."

"Nope. I doubt this will happen." She got up and started down the steps. "I'll call her in the morning."

"You're leaving?" I asked, trying not to let disappointment show in my voice.

"How do you feel about getting some Vietnamese at the Cuc Tran?" she asked.

"Count me in!" I usually cooked at home to save money, but a guy has to make allowances for evenings with a beautiful woman.

CHAPTER FIVE

***

It was a pleasant meal. Wenatchee, while the largest town in our area, still managed to maintain a certain charm that was lost in the contiguous cities in the western side of our state. Rosa and I had our favorites for dinner, then, to get some exercise, we made our way down to the waterfront park to take a stroll along the riverwalk.

The sun had gone down over an hour before, and it was late enough that the lights along the trail were flickering on. I could see that Rosa was pretty deep in thought.

"Graciella?" I asked.

She looked up, as if realizing we hadn't spoken in the last ten minutes. "What? Oh, Mac. Sorry, guess I'm not much in the inspiring conversation department. But yeah. Graciella."

"So, whatcha thinkin'?"

"It was just such a… weird visit, you know? She kept singing his praises, but something was off. Like it was all coached."

"Maybe she already knows he's an abuser," I said. "From personal experience."

"I just feel like giving her a call isn't enough, but I can't just barge in and tell her to get rid of him either." She looked toward the river. "I hate feeling helpless. It reminds me all too much of my childhood."

"It's possible that… Hey! Do you smell smoke?"

"We always smell smoke these days with all these huge

forest fires. Probably the wind has shifted again and it's coming down the canyon from the main fire complex," Rosa said. "Maybe…" She stopped in her tracks, then pointed up at one of the hillsides surrounding Wenatchee.

"Holy shit!" I said. "That looks like it's almost on the edge of town. Where the hell did that come from?"

"It is on the edge of town! There's a new development up there on a small plateau. Looks to me like the flames are coming from there."

I heard sirens. Flames were rocketing up from the site, and I realized my hope that no one else would be hurt by these fires was in vain. I started to see debris drift up into the atmosphere, flaming debris, in a county as dry as an old bone in the desert. I felt my gut clench with fear.

"Jeeze! Look, Mac," Rosa said as a flaming bit of what looked like paper landed on the lawn near us.

Not good. We were quite a bit down the valley from the fire, with a lot of residences and businesses between us and this new blaze.

A closer inspection revealed a partial word in blue as I stomped it out. It said. 'Tyve…" but the rest was singed.

Then I got it. Tyvek. The inner layer of material used to line new home construction.

People's homes were definitely burning.

As darkness moved in, Rosa and I hurried up past the local Office Depot, onto Wenatchee Avenue. Heading north in the general direction of the chaos, we both wanted to help, with no idea how we'd do so.

Instead, we wound up watching the climbing flames on the hill along with the growing crowd on the streets. Up at the fire, flashing blue and red lights could be seen reflecting off trees and buildings, and I was sure every available firefighter in the area was fighting like hell to contain the growing inferno.

"Rosa," I said, my worst-case scenario imagination kicking in, "what if that fire just keeps marching house to house the length of Wenatchee?" I imagined our small city becoming another Great Chicago Fire.

"No, they'll get it contained and…" Her words faded, and I realized she was staring not at the fire, but at the buildings behind the retail stores on our side of the road.

Smoke was rising from one of the fruit warehouses.

"Oh. My. God." she said. "Some of that flaming stuff's started another fire down here!"

Others saw where we were pointing and a chorus of frightened voices arose as people strove to make sense of what they were seeing. Rosa and I started in that direction, again wanting to help. With all the firefighters on the hill we hoped we could extinguish the flames before they took off. Rosa called 911 as we trotted toward the new fire.

By the time we covered the three blocks, the new fire was already beyond anything we could stop. A bin of what looked like recycled cardboard was blazing, and from fifty feet, it was hot enough on my face to make me not want to move a step closer. Though the warehouses were concrete, palettes were catching and the concrete wall of the building next to the bin looked like it was starting to deform.

Bits of flaming cardboard drifted into the sky, blowing toward the river, and I prayed they'd drop in the middle of the Columbia.

"Mac," I heard Rosa say with a strange tone in her voice, "we need to leave."

"Why, what…" She was pointing, and when I looked, I broke into a sweat that had nothing to do with the flames.

Propane tanks. Oh. Shit.

I wasn't sure what the fruit industry was using the propane for, and it didn't really matter. All that mattered was that there were multiple tanks around the warehouses, and some of them, by this time were undoubtedly getting very warm.

"We're moving, now," she said. We turned back the way we had come, and Rosa once again got on her cell to

RiverCom, but it was busy. Our 911 network was maxed out. "Mac, stop those people. I need to tell 911 what's going on, or the firefighters will walk into a time bomb!"

"Aw crap," Many of the people who had been watching the fire on Wenatchee Ave were making their way toward the warehouse fire to play sightseer. "No! No, people, you need to turn back, right now. That warehouse has tanks full of propane just waiting to…"

WAAHBOOM!

The first explosion rocked us all, causing several people to stagger. There was no need to guide the *touristas* away now. People began fast walking and in some smarter cases, running in the opposite direction. One notable exception, a photographer from the local paper, kept moving forward, camera in hand.

"Mike!" I yelled after him. "The shot's not worth your life, man!"

He turned for a moment and shrugged as if to say, "*Gotta do what I gotta do.*"

"God protects fools, little children and newspaper people," I said. "I hope."

"Mac, another warehouse," Rosa said, directing my attention from the photographer. "How are these concrete building catching fire? Oh… crap… they've got tar on the roofs, don't they?"

"That'd be my guess."

We heard sirens approaching. "I hope that means they have the neighborhood fire under control," Rosa said.

We heard a loud hissing sound behind us, and I saw the photographer running our way, camera carried like a football that didn't want to be fumbled.

"There's another one venting!" he yelled. "It's gonna…"

A loud explosion went off behind him, and he went down hard. It was a testament to his professionalism that he cradled his camera and took the impact to the asphalt himself rather than let his photo gear be broken. I ran over and helped him up and we all got the heck out of there.

***

The night was a long one. Booms from exploding tanks full of various chemicals punctuated the night on a regular basis, and I was glad I hadn't taken up firefighting as a profession. Those guys were definitely crazy-brave.

Around 1:00 a.m., the fires were controlled, and the local radio station said two warehouses were lost. The number was even worse for the neighborhood fire. Multiple houses burned to the ground, and the only good thing about it was no human lives were lost. Some pets, however didn't make it and there would be broken hearts in the morning.

As tired as we could be, Rosa returned to her apartment and I drove the Doom-mobile back to my trailer. It was indeed a long night, but it would be a longer morning for those who were getting a good look at their destroyed homes in the morning light.

One thing everyone agreed on though, we were all going to be damn glad when fire season ended.

CHAPTER SIX

***

The terrors of the previous night had ended, for most of the people in our area. The fires were out, and the work of cleaning up was probably already underway. I felt for the people whose homes had burned. I hoped that their fire insurance would cover what they needed to get their lives back.

While I could have done my research work from home the next morning, I called my uncle and told him I was coming out to his ranch later in the day. All four of the people on our team could log into the background-check sites that we and thousands of other investigative professionals use in our various trades, and I decided I wanted to be able to ask Melinda questions while I worked.

After getting off the phone, I stepped onto my deck with a cup of coffee to start my day right. Three seasons out of the year, I spent a goodly amount of time outside and not in my Airstream. Much as I loved my little simple trailer and the minimalist lifestyle I'd taken up, when you live in a tiny domicile, living part of your life outside actually makes sense. I'd rather have a small home on some land than a mansion on a postage-stamp lot any day of the week. I was, however, strongly contemplating an air conditioner.

After last night's flaming mess, I couldn't help but assess the possibility of fire here at my home, but the basalt cliffs behind me weren't very flammable, and the proximity to the river kept most of my oasis green. We'd done a good job of clearing the brush and grass around my mom's place too.

I heard splashing down at the river.

“Well, hello there,” I said quietly. The local otters were playing on my tiny beach area, chasing and rolling each other over when they caught their mates. Just being joyous in being alive. The people on this planet could learn a lot from otters. Thinking of all the pain people were going through right now, I wasn’t so sure otters could learn much of use from us.

I took the Doom-mobile up my steep driveway and along the dirt road toward the main highway. As I was passing my mom’s ranch-style house, she came out and waved me down.

“Are you going to Gilbert’s?” she asked.

“Yeah, Mom. I want to interview Melinda, that lady who lost her savings. I’ve only gotten a start going over her…”

“I want to go with you. Wait here a moment while I get my purse.”

I was wondering what was going on, when she came out, put her purse on the seat and said, “Let’s go.”

“What’s up, Mom?”

“We can talk about it when we get there.”

***

We drove through the Palisades Canyon on the way out to my uncle’s ranch. The basalt cliffs reminded me of photos I’d seen of the Southwest, but these had been carved by a huge flood, around 15,000 years ago. Isolated farms lined the sheer walls of the canyon, oases of green in a sea of rock and sagebrush. Taking Highway 2 through Waterville would have gotten me there faster, but I’ve always loved taking the scenic route.

My mother hadn’t said two words the entire trip so far, which was very much unlike her.

I came out of the north end of the canyon into open sagebrush and farm country. In one lonesome stretch of land there was a circular drive with small trailers like mine interspersed with RVs, some with solar panels. Most had a single vehicle in front, some with canvas carports. It was an incongruous thing to see out here, far from anything in a sea of sagebrush, but I thought I knew what had caused this little community to sprout up.

With the way the economy had tanked a few years ago, a lot of older folks like Melinda were living on tiny amounts of income in a world that just kept getting more expensive. Adopting minimalism for them was not a lifestyle choice; it was survival. It strengthened my resolve to help her find her money and shake it out of the jackal who'd taken it.

"Undeveloped land out here is fairly cheap," I said, gesturing toward the isolated trailers. "I'd bet that at least some of the people living here are seniors trying to get the most out of meager incomes. Lucky you've got a decent retirement plan through the hospital." Usually getting my mom to talk wasn't difficult.

"Yes, Mac. But I am a fair ways from being a senior yet, thank you very much."

"Yeah, I know. I was just commenting." She didn't reply.

We drove the back roads to my uncle's ranch, passing wheat fields and, on occasion, stretches of charred sagebrush and bunch grass. Burnt reminders of the lack of rain this summer.

"I was wondering when you'd get here," Melinda said, walking out the front door of the ranch house as we drove up. Evidently I wasn't the only one resolved to finding her money.

"Hi Melinda," I said. "Ready to help me do some digging?"

"Oh yeah," she said. "I was born ready. I hope we can get a lead on this guy. Even if I don't get back a cent, I really want him to go to jail."

As my mom got out of the truck Melinda's face changed to an odd expression.

"Hello there," she said. "Haven't we met?"

"Melinda," I said, "this is my mother, Joanne Crow."

"Hello, Melinda," Mom said, "Yes, we have met. Let's go inside and talk to Gil."

I was wondering what that was all about when I felt a tingle on the back of my neck.

I turned around to see the King, a large coyote who I'd had some… connections to in the past. Strange connections. He sat out in the sagebrush watching me. It may seem like a weird thing to do, but I nodded in acknowledgement. His head dipped slightly, he got to his feet and trotted into the brush.

That stuff was always a little unsettling.

"Wow," Melinda said, "did you see that big coyote? You'd think they'd be a bit more shy out here in ranch country."

"Not that one. He's not afraid of anything, far as I can tell. Note that we always keep the cat inside."

"Oh hell yeah," she said.

We walked inside, and I noted that Uncle Gil's worries that 'his owner' might not want another cat around were groundless. Cat-cat and Mr. McGow were curled up in a pretty good recreation of the Yin and Yang symbol on the sofa, leaving no room for doubt, nor room for anyone else to sit down.

"Where is everyone?" Mom asked.

"Gil and Ed went somewhere out thataway," Melinda told her. "Ed said someone's been driving four wheelers on your uncle's land without permission, trashing the place, and it's pissing him off. They went out to block off the route they're using."

"Ah. Yeah. He hates that." I sat at the computer desk in the study and turned the laptop on. It was less than a year old and top of the line. The farm itself looked old on the outside, but some fairly strong structural reinforcements had been made to the ranch house after the mercenary incident.

Even when business was slow, my uncle seemed to have the resources for such high-tech computer upgrades and defensive preparations. It had piqued my curiosity more than once, but I'd quickly learned not to ask. He'd made it clear it was none of my business.

I sat down and motioned for Melinda to sit beside me as I brought up some of my favorite skip-tracing sites.

"Can you tell me what kind of car he was driving?" I asked.

"A Lexus, nice and shiny new. Every item he had on him was expensive enough that the average working person wouldn't have bought it. His freakin' watch was a Rolex, and I doubt it was a fake. He made sure everyone at the seminar saw it."

I went into Carfax and inquired about vehicles. The reports listed that Johnson was based in Bend, Oregon.

Sure enough, I found a lease on a Lexus in his name. He'd failed to make his payment the month before he'd stopped sending his *clients'* payments, and a repo team had found the luxury car sitting in front of the home he'd been renting. They'd taken it.

"Just about everything I'm finding is temporary stuff," I said. "Nothing here looks like it was purchased, all rented or leased. Melinda, since you spoke with him personally, can you tell me anything that he might have said, just in passing, small talk maybe, that might be useful?"

"Aaaah! I'll try." She thought for a moment, replaying old conversations in her head while I looked for background info on some of Johnson's other aliases. "When he came to see me, he talked about the benefits, the pie-in-the-sky benefits that his program would bring me. He didn't really talk that much about himself. He mostly had me talking about me."

"Like any good stage magician," Mom said. I looked back at her, hearing a bitter tone. She looked out the window at the rolling fields.

"You have to understand, Mac," Melinda said, nodding at Mom's comment, "there was something almost mesmerizing about him. When I was a young girl, I got to spend about fifteen minutes in the company of a famous and very handsome star, and he charmed everyone in the room completely. He was totally on. It was the same with Jori Johnson, famous or not."

"Oh, I know what you're talking about. Had a jerk like that ruin my life for a while."

Melinda looked at me, expectantly, and I realized I'd opened the door for her to pry into the story. I sighed.

"When I was a teen, I was put in a wilderness/nature school called the Seeker School. My life was pretty good there except for one kid, Frank Batteau. When I was sixteen, I had a girlfriend, also a student at the school, named Kailee, and Batteau wanted her. He began instigating fights with me and if no one was around, being bigger, he'd soundly stomp me. I wasn't the sort to go cry to the instructors so he got away with it. If I did complain, he was so good at manipulating them that I'd almost always come out with the dirty end of the stick."

"I sense there's more," Melinda said.

"As I mentioned he wanted my girl, he needed me out of the way. Our last fight, came suddenly, just out of the sight of the staff, and he smacked me hard in the back, laughing about it. At that point, I had SO had it with the guy I just went kinda feral, which totally played into his hands. For some reason I was doing a LOT better than usual, and managed to nail him several times in the face. Then he started screaming like I'd torn off his finger or something. He flopped onto his back just as the instructors showed up and begged them to help him, that I'd gone nuts and was trying to kill him."

"Was he badly hurt?"

"Black eye, split lip, maybe, but he wrapped his arms around his middle, claiming I'd been kicking him. I saw he'd smeared dirt on his midsection before he'd even started things. That's about when I knew something was up. Of course, they listened to him and I was made to look like a damn psycho. The school kicked me out."

"Oh, dear."

"I was gone. He wound up with my girl and later married

her, unhappily for us both. She divorced him last year," I said. "You know the funny thing, though?"

"Tell me, Mac."

"I kinda owe him. Without Frank, I wouldn't be in karate, would never have met Ed, and wouldn't be with Rosa."

"Why," she said, almost laughing, "he's your George Baily!"

"With an Old Man Potter personality."

I sat for a moment, lost in memories of things that shouldn't have happened. My mom gently laid her hand on my shoulder. She'd seen all I went through and the pain of losing what I thought was everything at the time.

"Well," I said. "Back to it."

Almost all of Johnson's other aliases led to the same place, Nothingville. Most times when we were skip-tracing felons, they were of lesser intelligence or not as savvy about hiding their tracks. Our man Jori however was well aware that any truthful info he gave could help people track him down, and was meticulous at leaving disinformation wherever he went.

I checked the sites of the funds he had placed on Melinda's statement, and all were legitimate. It was the URL for his own company, whose individual pages were supposed to show the client their shares and dividends, that came up *domain for sale*.

He'd used legitimate mutual funds that he was never actually involved with to convince his victims.

Melinda scanned the *domain for sale* message on the laptop's screen. "That's new. I checked those about a month ago, and the pages were still there. I'm not that good with the web."

"My guess is that whatever you were directed to, it would have looked both rosy and convincing. It's all too easy to lie on the Internet," I said. "The sick thing is, as well as lying about this stuff, he must've had some experience as a broker. A guy this smart probably could have made a decent living at it without screwing people."

"But he might not have gotten rich quick," Mom said, an edge of bitterness in her voice that I hadn't heard before.

"Now I know where I saw you, Joanne. You were at Jori's seminar in Wenatchee, weren't you?" Melinda said.

You could have knocked me over with a feather.

Oh shit.

"And all of us he screwed didn't matter. We weren't people. We were just resources." Mom said.

"Oh Mom, no…"

"Yes." My mother looked down at the floor, deep embarrassment in her expression. "And when your uncle hears it, he's going to go nuts."

"How much?" I almost didn't want to know.

"My entire 401(k) from the hospital, around one hundred and ten thousand. Everything except the 5% matched funds from my employer," She said. "I thought I could get a halfway decent dividend without touching my principal. I was going to apply the dividend to my mortgage payment each month, and my retirement wouldn't shrink. Now I'll also get a big tax bill, to add insult to injury."

"Oh honey," Melinda said. "I feel your pain. I lost over three hundred thousand with no way to make more retirement funds."

"At least I'm still employed."

"And you can't be much past fifty. You still have some time to recoup." Melinda told her.

"Yeah, but it's gonna be a skimpy retirement. With the mortgage on that ranch of ours, we are stretched thin. It was only Mac's last bounty hunting job that paid the mortgage this month."

I was feeling sick to my stomach. Not only had the bastard bilked Melinda, but he'd harmed my mom's financial future. Mine, too. I understood mom's reluctance to tell Uncle Gil. He could sometimes be abrasive when he was irritated, and had little sympathy when people screwed up.

He didn't know about this yet, but when he found out, if he tried to bury her under a mound of abuse, he was going to be shut down quick. He was several years older than my mother, and tended to treat her like the little sister still.

But if we'd known earlier, the trail wouldn't have become so cold.

"Well, Mom," I said, "I guess when we get Melinda's money back, we'll just have to squeeze yours out of him as well."

"You raised a pretty good son here, Joanne."

"I like to think so. If I could only convince him to be more careful."

"So," I said. "The seminar was just a little over a year ago. Mom, did you talk to him much?"

"Just over a lunch meeting. That was all it took to convince me, and I wasn't savvy enough to know ways to check on his claims," she said. "And yes, I realize now I should have gone to Gil or you to do a background check. Lesson learned the hard way."

There was no point in commenting, so I just moved on.

"I wonder if any of the other victims got him to talk about himself. I have so little real info to get traction with here."

Mel sat up straight, looking out over the sagebrush, through the one large picture window in the house. "There was… oh, what was his name?"

"Melinda? What?"

"Many of the victims met, in Las Vegas. It was where we all chipped in for the investigators. As you might guess, we spent a lot of time commiserating with each other and I talked to a man who was even angrier about Johnson than the rest of us. Impassioned. Ballistic, you might say. Said he'd invited Johnson to go out on his sailboat with him, and they'd all talked for hours."

"Sounds like someone I'd *really* like to interview."

***

Melinda's contact was named Gavin Thomas, and it took my cross referencing of her victim group mailing list with a few web searches to find a way to reach him.

"You're sure this is the guy?" I asked.

"I'm pretty sure," she said, "There was a lot of mutual misery at this meeting, and I struck up a conversation with this man. He told me that he'd spent a fair amount of time with Johnson, because they both loved to be out on the water. He thought he and Johnson had developed sort of a friendship, and he was pretty bitter about the whole thing, even more than most of us."

"If I get him on the phone, can you verify it's him? If it is, we might learn something, some hook we need just through talking to him."

Uncle Gil still had a landline, and I used that to make the call. Such a phone was old school, but calls wouldn't cut in and out as they sometimes did with cell phones out here.

"Ringing," I said. "Hello? Is this Mister Thomas? No, sir, not selling anything or asking for any money. My name is Mac Crow and… no, sir, not Macro. Mac, MacKenzie. Yes, sir, you're not the first one to make that witty observation." I couldn't help but roll my eyes. "Mr. Thomas, I am representing Melinda Smythe, and trying to find information on the man you know as Jori Johnson."

The phone went silent.

"Sir," I continued, "I believe you spoke with Ms. Smythe at the meeting of Johnson's victims in Vegas. She's here with me now. Would you like to speak with her? Okay. Do you mind if I put you on speaker? Thank you."

I hit the correct button and returned the phone to its cradle. Thomas's voice came from the speaker. "Can you hear me okay?"

"Yes," Melinda said, slightly overloud, "Gavin, this is Melinda. Do you remember me?"

"Of course. You and my daughter Laurie got into that long conversation about cats."

Melinda gave me a thumbs up. This was the man we needed to talk to.

"Mr. Thomas, you and Melinda talked, and you told her you had spent a fair amount of time with Johnson and gotten to know him a bit. We're looking for any lead we can find to bring this guy in."

"Melinda," Thomas said, "what exactly is your connection with Mister Crow?"

"Gavin, I'm pretty much destitute. A forest fire wiped out my home, and Mac and his uncle took me in and put a roof over my head. It was coincidence that they're bounty hunters, but sometimes things happen for a reason."

"Sometimes, things happen because people make them happen. Tell you what, Mister Crow. You want to interview me, you can do it face to face. I'm a little less inclined to trust people at face value these days, and even less so over the phone. Where are you located?"

"We're in Wenatchee, in Washington."

"Not sure where that is…"

"About a hundred miles east of Seattle."

"Well, I'm in Seaside, Oregon and I'm willing to meet you for coffee. I'd like to size you up face to face. Bring Melinda."

"All right," I said, stifling an inner sigh. "When and where?"

"There's a Starbuck's on South Roosevelt. Can you be here by tomorrow afternoon?"

"We'll make it happen. How about 3:00 p.m.?"

"Sounds good." Before he hung up, we traded cell numbers and said our goodbyes.

I looked at Melinda. "Now we just have to sell this trip to Uncle Gil."

"I'll handle that," Mom said.

CHAPTER SEVEN

***

I'd been surprised. Uncle Gil hadn't yelled at my mom, hadn't tried to give far-too-late lessons on not being defrauded and swindled. He actually listened, which was NOT something I was used to.

After she told him her story, it wasn't difficult to talk my uncle into the use of *Non-Descript,* the older model Acura we used for surveillance.

"Mac, you take Melinda and Rosa and go have a talk with this Thomas guy. The company will pay for gas and a room for all of you." He'd said, "Your mom and I will get things sorted out here." I was glad to not be part of that conversation, but I pulled him aside.

"Listen Uncle Gil," I said. "Do NOT give Mom a big ration of shit. She feels badly enough about this."

"Don't intend to," he said, a pained expression on his face. "Everyone screws up big-time once in a while, Mac, as you well know."

I left it at that. I wasn't sure which of my personal screw-ups he was referring to and really didn't want to know. The next day, Mel, Rosa and I were on our way to the Oregon coast.

We'd just left I-5 before taking the bridge into Oregon. The road out towards Longview was a scenic byway that was part of a long string of scenic byways. Now, driving along the Columbia River near the end of its run to the Pacific Ocean, I hoped this wasn't going to turn into a wild goose chase.

"This is such a beautiful drive," Rosa commented from

behind me. "Why haven't we done this before?"

"You two kids think this is nice," Melinda said from the passenger seat, "wait 'til we get to the Oregon coast proper! Oh! Mac, rest area, can we stop?"

"Sure," I said, pulling into the picturesque little bathroom/ picnic ground.

"It's so... damp... along here," Rosa said. "It's so dry where we live. I love all these ferns, and all this moss on the rocks here on the shoreline. It's like something out of a fairy tale."

As I watched, a salmon jumped about twenty yards from the shore. The Columbia was one of the biggest salmon rivers in the world, but overfishing by huge trawlers in the ocean, both foreign and domestic, had cut the number of salmon that made it upstream substantially. I was always glad to be reassured that salmon still swam here.

"Haven't I ever taken you over into the forests near North Bend? It's a lot like this, though much smaller rivers."

"Can't say that you ever have. Try to rectify that, okay?"

"I promise."

"Oh, dear God," Melinda said walking back from the bathroom. "That is so much better. I envy you young people. I seem to have the bladder of a hamster these days."

"No worries here," I said. "But that hamster might be getting miffed about you taking his bladder."

"Funny, Mr. Comedian."

"Forgive him, Melinda," Rosa said. "He thinks he's a wit, when he's only half of one."

"I aims to please," I said.

Back in the car, we eventually ran out of continent and took a left onto the Astoria–Megler Bridge, a huge metal beam cantilevered structure that joined Washington and Oregon near the mouth of the Columbia. As we started across, one of the thick fog banks that often form in the area engulfed us. In a short time, we couldn't see more than twenty feet ahead, nothing but bridge and mist.

“Well, this is eerie,” Rosa said.

“I keep expecting to see angels flying alongside of us,” Melinda said.

“Hopefully, we haven’t taken a left turn,” I said, “INTO THE TWILIGHT ZONE!”

“Do do do do…” Rosa started singing the old theme song, but quickly stopped. “Actually, I’m freaking myself out here.”

The fog dissipated as we came off the bridge near the coastal town of Astoria, one of Oregon’s oldest communities. Turning right on highway 101, we headed south. The drive down the Oregon coast is pretty incredible, and not to be missed. We passed through sleepy towns, now filled with tourists, lighthouses, incredible headland rock formations, and beautiful beaches of rock and sand. Glancing back and seeing Rosa stare out the window like a kid in a candy store gave me no small amount of pleasure.

“The last time I was down here, I was still married,” Melinda said.

“Did something happen to your husband?” I asked.

“Sure did. I sent him packing. He was one of those people who could never bear to be wrong, so if he was, he argued until everyone else just shut up. Which was what he wanted. After the kids moved out, I realized I was married to someone who irritated the hell out of me and that I didn’t have to stay married to him.” She sighed. “Unfortunately, both my son and daughter seemed to have inherited some of his traits. Our relationship is… strained.”

“Aii…” Rosa said. “No bueno.”

“Don’t miss him, but I don’t see our children often enough. Pains in the butt though they can be, they’re still my kids.”

We rolled into Seaside around 2:30 pm. It was a beautiful little town, seemingly quiet until one noted the large beach which was doing a brisk business in tourism. It took me a while to find a parking spot, and then we had to backtrack on foot to the local Starbucks, passing little tourist beach trinket shops along the way.

We walked into the coffee shop, and I scanned for Gavin Thomas. Going through our skip-tracing sites, I'd obtained his photo from his driver's license. He was sitting in a corner, holding down a four-person table and watching the tourists walk by.

"Mr. Thomas?" I asked. He stood, and introductions were conducted all around. Thomas was somewhere in his mid-sixties, trim and in shape. His graying hair hadn't gone white but his tanned face held the lines of a man who liked to spend as much time outdoors as possible. I got us all coffee while Rosa and Melinda broke the ice. When I returned and took my seat, Melinda led off.

"Gavin, I appreciate you taking the time to talk to Mac and Rosa. I want you to know they are serious about finding Jori Johnson and bringing him to justice."

"So," Thomas said, appearing to size me up in his mind, "bounty hunter, eh? That pay well?"

"It can, assuming you survive."

"You seem pretty young for that trade. Why'd you want to talk to me, specifically? You interviewing anyone else in our group?"

"I'm not by any means ruling that out. From my conversation with Melinda, I've got a suspicion that Johnson spent more time shining people on by getting them to talk about themselves and their families than he did talking about himself. That, of course, and the ever-present sales pitch."

He nodded.

"Melinda tells me that you spent a little time with the man, taking him sailing out on your boat. If you spent that much time together…"

"We all make mistakes," he said with bitterness. "But

yeah, we did talk quite a bit," Thomas said. "But there was more than that."

I waited.

"He's a… very attractive man, in his own way."

"I see," I said, realizing what Thomas was telling me. "Maybe that's even better, more opportunities for an unguarded moment?"

He seemed to relax then, my not showing judgment of his personal life appearing to set him a bit at ease.

"I'd originally not been inclined to see him, when he first came to me with his grandiose dividend plan, but if you'd ever met him, you'd know why I let him in. Jori… Jordan could have worked for the CIA and they'd never have to use drugs or torture in an interrogation again. They could have just sent their prisoners out to coffee with him and by mid-afternoon there'd be no secrets left."

"So, how'd you know he was…?" Rosa asked.

"Gay?" Thomas laughed a soft laugh. "I assure you, my 'gaydar' is well tuned, much moreso than most. I know, for instance that you are not playing for my team, Mr. Crow."

"Oh?"

"Oh yes," he said, a mischievous sparkle coming to his eyes. "Every since this young lady sat down with us, a part of your attention, no matter how much you are concentrating on what I'm saying, is always on her."

I could feel my face redden, though I wasn't sure why. I turned to Rosa, who was grinning and couldn't help but laugh.

"All right. Point taken," I said. "Did you invite him out on your boat? Or did he wrangle an invite?"

"I invited him. I'm by no means the only gay person in this town, but I sometimes feel that way. And to be honest, Jordan is pretty hot. I was overjoyed when he said yes, and only later did he confide his love for the ocean."

"That could be something."

"I have to be honest," Thomas said. "I'm as susceptible as anyone to being flattered, and I did most of the talking also, at his urging. Still, there comes a point when any decent person will take the topic of conversation off themselves, and try to get the person they're with to open up."

It might have been my imagination, but Melinda seemed to sink into her chair a little.

"And did Johnson get any more specific about his love for the ocean? Anything from his past that we can get some traction on?" I asked.

Thomas nodded. "Evidently, he was a surfer kid when he was younger, and I got the impression that he grew up on one of the islands. Though I doubt his name then was Jori Johnson."

"Hawaii, then?" Melinda asked.

"Yes, but I have no idea which island. But… he mentioned something about growing up in the shadow of Elvis's hotel. I've not been to any of the islands except Maui, myself, but that seems pretty specific."

"That could help us a lot. If we can find out which island, we might find out what his real name is. If we have that, we can learn a crap ton of possible ways to track him," Rosa told him.

The rest of the interview was pretty much us trying to help Gavin Thomas rack his brain to come up with any tidbit of pertinent information that we could use. There were a few vague leads, but nothing as solid as the Hawaii trail. After an hour, we thanked him, and I gave him my number in case he thought of anything else.

"Mr. Crow, a favor?" he asked.

"What can I do for you?"

"My… wife knows about my… being gay. We've been together as best friends for many years, and I'd appreciate it if my preferences were kept quiet, more for her sake, than mine," he said. "I love her, and I don't want her to be judged in any way."

"Our lips are sealed."

"Thank you."

Rosa, Melinda and I left and headed back to the car. Next stop was the little cottage I'd rented for the night.

"Blue Hawaii," Melinda said.

"That the Elvis Hawaii movie?" I asked.

"Yes, but damn if I can remember which island it was shot on. It's been so long since I've seen it."

"There were three Elvis Hawaii movies, according to Wikipedia," Rosa said, looking at her phone as she walked. "If the hotel is the one from Blue Hawaii, it's the Coco Palms Resort on the east coast of Kauai, now abandoned. There's also a hotel scene at Hilton Hawaiian Village on Waikiki Beach on Oahu."

"That narrows it down to two islands, and from what I've gleaned, Johnson is somewhere between thirty and thirty-five years old. We may have a solid lead here."

"One can hope."

***

We drove to the little cottage we were staying at, down a moss-covered side street and let our selves in. None of the three of us had brought much more than overnight bags. We were all used to traveling light. It was a smallish little cabin, well-kept but slightly musty smelling. I guessed that no matter what time of year, in a place as wet as this, it always smelled that way.

"I don't know about you two kids," Melinda said, "but I am bushed after that long drive. I think I'll take a nap before we go looking for a place to have dinner."

"Mac," Rosa said, "let's go take a walk on the beach. I never got to walk along the ocean shore before."

"But we've been on the waterfront in Seattle, more than once…?"

She looked at me like I was thick in the head. "Really? You're going to compare a smelly pier with this wonderful beach with all those big rocks out there?"

"Point taken. Melinda, you gonna be okay here?"

"I've managed for all these years," she said, smiling. "I guess I can get along without your company for a few hours. You two go do some living."

Rosa and I headed down the narrow backstreet until we came to a small trail between houses that read "Public Beach Access" and vectored toward the sound of the waves. A cool breeze blew in off the Pacific as we walked arm in arm, and I was silently warmed to see how much Rosa was enjoying herself.

The love of my life is usually all business, very competent, and not one to be trifled with. Today, she was a kid, eyes looking everywhere with joy and enthusiasm. She stopped for a moment and pointed at a sign on a post. It read *Tsunami Evacuation Route*.

"Tsunami!" she exclaimed in mock fear. "Oh lordy, we gonna die!"

"Don't worry, kid," I said. "I'll sling ya over one shoulder and run like the wind."

"Who you callin' kid?" she replied, the all-knowing eyebrow raised. "And I'm pretty sure I can run faster than you."

"Cool, grannie, then you can sling me over your shoulder."

She spent a few moments posing and flexing then we continued down to the beach.

"So," I said. "Kauai or Oahu. Might be a decent lead."

"Maybe. When we get home, we can go to that yearbook site and see what we can come up with," Rosa replied. "Even if we find him as a kid, and get a lead on his real identity and family members, it's no guarantee we'll be able to trace Johnson through them."

"You never know. Sometimes parents feel shame when their kid turns out to be a lying piece of shit."

"Or sometimes the kids turn out like crap because the parents are crap," she said, her brows knitting with the thought of some old memory.

"All I know is, when we find Johnson, he might have a few extra lumps and bruises on him before we run him in. The rat bastard," I said, thinking of the shamed look on my mom's face.

"Hmmm. Maybe we could arrange an unfortunate fall down a flight of stairs."

"Wouldn't break my heart."

"He's sure put your mom in a bind."

"I've been thinking, Rosa. I've been paying Mom for my portion of the mortgage, but maybe I need to take out a loan and buy my part of the property from her outright. I love my mom, but this kinda freaked me out."

"Since it's not your land, per se," Rosa asked, "and you hardly own anything, what you gonna use to get the loan?"

"I've managed to save some, when times were good. Uncle Gil's been diverting money from our paychecks to retirement accounts too, so I was thinking I might be able to convince a loan officer to back me."

"Might take some of the strain off your mom, too. Less land that Joanne needs to pay on, and the part you buy could help her out if we don't recover her money…"

I happened to be looking out over the ocean when I saw the car gunning down the beach. We weren't directly in its path, but nudging Rosa, we both backed out of the way. Several other beach walkers had to hot step to clear its path and numerous middle fingers were raised as the older model Ford blasted past.

"I'm pretty sure there was a sign back there that said not to drive on the beach," I said.

"Look at who's driving, some rebels-sans-clues."

The car had two shaggy-haired teens in it, who were happily

returning obscene gestures to everyone they passed, right up until they drove on the edge of the surf and stopped abruptly. A few moments later, the sound of spinning tires not gaining traction came to us over the sound of the waves. A slow smile spread across our faces, and the faces of most people walking near us.

"Gee, Rosa, looks like the tide's coming in pretty fast."

"Oh no. How awful."

"It is, isn't it?"

We sat on a log and watched as one of the teens got out and desperately tried to push the back of the car. The surf came in to his knees and as the tires spun, he got a face-full of sand and sea water. No one on the beach tried to aid them. Some might take that as being callous, but it was really that everyone was happy to see a much needed lesson learned.

"Ooo! That wave looks like it splashed into the window," Rosa said.

"I'm thinkin' they're going to have to gift that car to Poseidon." The two teens however, were frantically trying to fight the rising tide and save the car and the tide was rising fast. I kicked off my shoes.

"Oh, you're not…"

"I don't think their IQ is high enough to realize that their lost cause is starting to get dangerous."

Others along the beach were starting to look concerned also, and a few were starting to yell to the boys to clear off. They weren't listening. I hit the surf-line and cold salt water splashed up my leg, not improving my mood.

"It's done! Your ride's sunk! Time to abandon ship!"

"I can't," the taller boy shouted back at me. "This is my dad's car. He'll fuckin' kill me, man! Can you help?"

"If I had another hour and a shovel, maybe. Right now, it's a done deal. Come in with me and start thinking of the excuses you'll use, 'cause your folks'd much rather lose this car than lose you."

The other boy thought about it for about two seconds then pushed through the rising waves toward shore.

"Tom!" the first boy yelled after his companion.

"Sorry man, but the dude's right! Car ain't worth bein' swept out to sea."

"Fucker! You're only sayin' that cause it ain't your car or your ass that's gonna get barbecued!"

"Hey. Look! Waves are already slappin' the engine," I said. "You can't save the Titanic here. Let's go."

The boy looked mournfully at the car, and a big wave came in and almost knocked us both off our feet. That was all the convincing it took and we waded in to a dry part of the beach. I walked over to Rosa, water running down my pants and sand sticking to everything wet.

"Poetic justice, I guess," she said, watching the teens trudge, heads down, toward the village. "Hopefully an omen of justice in the search for our creep."

"Works for me."

CHAPTER EIGHT

***

Our search for Johnson took a backseat when we returned home. Rosa, Melinda and I had rolled into Uncle Gil's ranch late that evening, having gotten off from Seaside late that day. We slept over.

Rosa and I were up early the next day, getting in a morning run on a well-worn game trail that traversed the property. Our route came out in a long sagebrush canyon that was open to public usage. The canyon ran for several miles, along a meandering stream filled with beaver dams.

"Starting to warm up already," I said as we trotted along.

"The better to get a good sweat going," she replied. "I wish this road was a little less rocky though."

"It'll give us tough ankles."

"Or a good sprain."

We'd done about four miles, when Rosa's phone, which she had attached to her armband with some sort of Velcro strap, buzzed.

"Huh," I said, "That's why I leave my phone back at the house when I'm running."

"Oh Mac, I would, but I'm just so much more important than…" Rosa frowned at her device. "It's Graciella. I need to take this." Rosa sat on a big basalt stone that was near the road and I walked down to the creek to give her some space.

I got to the water's edge, eyeing the tall grass for possible camping bedding. I kept one ear open for the sound of rattlesnakes.

The beavers had been busy. We were in high sagebrush desert country, and there was only so much area for beavers to move to, so they had colonized every bit of the canyon, making it a dropping series of ponds filled with small trout. What logically should have been an almost dry environment had become a grassy miles-long oasis.

I had once camped along this very creek, and when the beavers figured out where I was, they loudly splashed a couple times every hour, as if determined to keep me awake. I didn't sleep much that night, but out here away from the towns, the stars had been incredible.

Looking over my shoulder, I saw Rosa gesturing to the air angrily.

"Oh, that's not good," I said to myself. I had a sneaking suspicion that I knew what she was so angry about, and shared her frustration if I was right.

A glint caught my eye from downstream and I walked that way, watching the small trout chase each other. Getting to where I had seen the flash of light, I was disappointed to find cans and broken bottles strewn across what would have been a nice campsite. The mess was something you find in almost any pretty place you can drive to that isn't under some kind of supervision.

Pig people. I sighed and resolved to drive back with a big heavy-duty garbage bag.

Shell casings littered the ground, most of them .44s. The remains of several targets were all around the site. While I waited, I picked up the shell casings and put them in the pocket of my water bottle holder which was slung around my waist. Uncle Gil was teaching me to reload used ammo, and I was pretty sure he had the needed gear to reload this caliber.

"What's the word?" I asked as Rosa walked up. The stormy look on her face told me the news wasn't good.

"She called me up, all in tears. Guess why."

"Martinelli."

"Yup. Smacked her hard enough to knock a tooth loose, and she's evidently got a nice shiner to boot. I guess now she's listening to what I had to say to her."

I hated men who hit women, and I would have loved nothing better than to take David Martinelli into a back alley somewhere to use him as my personal Everlast bag.

"So, what's your play?"

"She's packing a small bag, I'm going down, and I'll text her when I get there. She'll slip out and I'm going to bring her back here."

"Sounds involved. Why doesn't she just call the cops?"

"For some reason, she wants me to come get her instead. Even fools have some primitive survival instincts, Mac."

"If you say so," I said. "When do we leave?"

"I'm going alone," she said. "I can handle this by myself. You'd just make her more edgy."

"Maybe, but I can also watch your back. This guy could be dangerous."

"I can handle it. I'm perfectly capable of protecting myself, Mac."

"I could take my old truck and shadow you. Graciella wouldn't ever need to know about…"

"I can handle it, Mac."

"So we're not even going to talk about it? You're risking your life and I don't have any input?"

Rosa looked at me like I had said something astonishing. "You sure don't."

The astonishment was mutual.

"*Dammit, Rosa!* Even the police have partners. Gil wouldn't let you go out without a partner, and you wouldn't question him."

"He's my boss. You're *not*."

"Really? What is this crazy thing, throwing yourself into

danger? Maybe you and Graciella have that in common."

She looked at me like *you didn't just go there*. But she wasn't one to stay silent. "Are you saying it's because we're Latinas?"

She was fuming now and so was I. She was throwing herself into danger to make a point. Well then, I was going to make mine.

"Not at all. I have no idea why you are acting like a nut case. That's what I'm trying to find out."

Okay, maybe, I shouldn't have said that.

The silence was deafening. Soon, there was the sound of birds and running water, but Rosa and I just stared at each other. I wasn't backing down if she was going to take unnecessary risks—just as she wouldn't with me.

"I. Will. Handle. It."

"Fine," I said, turning down the canyon. "Good luck."

I continued my run without her.

***

When I got back to the ranch house, the company Acura was gone. My old truck was parked in front of the barn and I tossed my sweaty shirt onto the passenger seat.

"Headin' out?" a gravelly voice said from the porch. I turned to see Uncle Gil leaning against a support post for the porch, drinking coffee. "Got time for a cuppa coffee?"

Part of me, still pissed at Rosa, just wanted to tear off down the road. But it was rare that my uncle wanted to talk in any capacity other than work, so I decided I needed a cup of something hot. Returning to the porch with a steaming mug, I sat near him at the slightly rusty deck dining set.

"Saw Rosa come back a little bit ago. She didn't look too happy." Uncle Gil went right to the point.

"I told her she was being crazy," I said. "She didn't seem to like that."

"What a surprise. What's she being crazy about?"

"She's got an unpleasant chore, down in the Tri-Cities."

We sat a moment, both looking out over the sage brush and wheat field. When I didn't elaborate, he continued.

"Hmm. Couldn't help but notice she kept looking back the direction you two went running. Looked kinda miserable, if I'm to be honest. I'd guess you two had a fight?"

"Not much of a fight," I said, looking down into my cup. "I offered to back her up on her chore. She informed me my help wasn't needed. I disagreed. She got pissed. Here we are."

"One thing I learned in the military, fights don't have to be long to be intense." He sipped his coffee. "What's this chore?"

I considered a moment how much I could tell Uncle Gil without making matters worse. Rosa wouldn't want me sharing too much of her personal business without her knowing, but I was worried that she was putting herself in danger by being stubborn. Her safety came ahead of any personal concerns. I must have deliberated almost five seconds before spilling the beans.

"Her friend down in Richland is with a shit-heel who's starting to beat on her. Rosa's going to retrieve said friend, and bring her back here, supposedly out of harm's way. I wanted to go as back-up, but for some reason, Rosa wouldn't accept my help."

"This guy know who Rosa is?"

"Her friend," I said, "is not the brightest bulb on the tree as far as I can tell, and probably not that discreet, so… who knows."

We both sat a while, listening to the general quiet of the countryside.

"I know advice from your grumpy uncle may not be what you're looking for, Mac, but if I was you, I'd make contact with Rosa. Text her. She's smart enough not to text and drive. If she's switched cars, she's got that phone stand in her RAV. Just send something brief, to let her know that comms are open. Staying mad is just a good way for both of you to be miserable. Believe me on this one."

I nodded.

"The other thing you might consider, when you talk to her, is to let her and her friend bunk out at your place for a while. Might be harder for a nasty boyfriend to find than Rosa's apartment."

"There's one other thing," I said. "This guy has a bench warrant out for his arrest."

"You don't say. Even better." My uncle scratched his stubbly chin. "If this fellow comes looking, could be he just might get his ass arrested, especially if he went looking for Rosa at her apartment. If Rosa wasn't involved, and you weren't more than peripherally involved… Ah well, sorry. I just like to meddle too much."

"Just planting seeds, Uncle Gil?"

"Well, son," he said, gesturing out over the wheat field to the south. "we ARE on a farm."

CHAPTER NINE

***

I was almost home when a ping came over my phone, denoting an incoming text. I had sent a brief note to Rosa before leaving Uncle Gil's, saying only, "You okay?"

Her reply, though it had taken an hour, made the tightness in my chest loosen a bit. *"Yeah. Call you in a while, Ok?"*

Back at my place, I went into the trailer and took my laptop out on the deck. As rustic as my location and trailer were, my WiFi router was the best money could buy, courtesy of Chambers and Associates. I logged on and began surfing the net even as I watched the waters of the Columbia roll by.

I pulled up a site I'd used a couple of times, one that had taken on the herculean task of scanning and making available every high school yearbook produced in the U.S. since the sixties. While they didn't provide much on the people we tracked for current information, they sometimes provided clues to other people that we could contact to find our flight risks.

There is a fair amount of difference between a teenager and the same person in their thirties. Most people tend to fill out more than their younger selves, or in some cases, they tend to lose weight as "baby fat" melts away. I had two possible advantages with Jordan Johnson, the first being that his hair was so blond it was almost white. The second was in his facial structure. Johnson had one of those wide symmetrical jaws, coming almost to a point at the chin. He had fairly prominent cheekbones, full lips, and had his features been just a little less pronounced, he'd have been movie star handsome.

Estimating his age range, I needed to go through several years in either direction. If what Johnson had told Gavin Thomas was true, and not another layered lie, then this might be possible. Fortunately for me, we had his past narrowed down to two islands.

"I seriously underestimated how long this is going to take," I said to myself an hour later. I had carefully scanned through four years of yearbooks for Oahu. The nearest to Waikiki was Kaimuki High School, which was where I was assuming the Hilton Hawaiian Village was, one of the two hotels used in Blue Hawaii. However, there were several high schools in Honolulu and none of them were so far apart that a student couldn't have been transferred to them for whatever reason.

"Why the hell am I doing this alone? I should let Melinda look through this stuff." I picked up my phone. "Hey, Uncle Gil. No. She hasn't called, but she texted me and said she'd call soon, so hopefully she's safe. Hey, can I get you to do something for me? Can you set Melinda up on the yearbook site and have her scan through the year books of the high school nearest the Coco Palms Resort? I think the town is Kapaa… Yeah, on Kauai. I'm looking on Honolulu. She'll know what years to scan. Great. This is taking more time than I thought, and I could use the help."

I also need a break to think.

After talking to my uncle, I went into the trailer and retrieved the little canvas haversack that I often carried when I went on walks. I stuffed my phone down into the folds of the cotton bandana inside and set off down river. Nothing helps clear the head like a long walk in a beautiful place.

I have two modes of travel outdoors. The first one is getting from point A to point B, whether trail running or hiking, I try to make good time while staying as aware of what is going on as I can.

The second one would try the patience of a saint. This is

"see everything" mode, and it can sometimes take two hours to move a mile.

I was in mode two, examining deer tracks at the downriver end of my property. Looking downstream, I saw the three old houses along the river, derelict, dilapidated and sitting forlorn. I'd always been curious about them but I was a little unclear of exactly where the property boundary was and people in Eastern Washington were very serious about trespassers. I resolved to get proper boundary maps of the place next time I was in the county courthouse.

I noted that the left rear track of the deer I was trailing had a slight offset when my haversack rang.

"Hey," the voice of my favorite person rose from my phone, "we're at the rest stop along the Columbia, heading up toward Desert Aire. Graci is in the women's can, so we can talk straight for a few minutes."

"How'd it go?"

"Not so good. Graci was almost to the car when Martinelli came storming out of the apartment building, running after her, screaming threats. She got so flustered she dropped her phone, and almost dropped her overnight bag. We gunned out of the parking lot, but my RAV now has a nice dent in the left rear panel from his fist."

"Are you okay?" I was tempted to say that I wished I had been there, but my self-preservation instincts kicked in and I stopped myself.

"Yeah, but swear to God, I wanted to stop at the end of the parking lot, let him catch us and put about ten rounds from my Glock into his sorry self."

"Probably best that didn't happen."

"Yeah. I don't look good in orange," Rosa said.

"Did he follow you?"

"For about five minutes, but I lost his piece o' crap low-rider Honda with a few little turns and maneuvers."

Rosa and I had needed to tail flight risks on several occasions. You learned a few things about how to lose a tail, whether you wanted to or not.

“That’s good,” I said. “So, you got away okay?”

“Maybe, however, I think he knows who I am, and probably the city I live in.”

“Oh Christ, she didn’t…”

“Yeah. Little Miss Loose Lips was telling Martinelli what a bad-ass bounty hunter I was, and how he’d better be nice to her or he could wind up in jail. Needless to say, that blew up in her face.”

“Quite literally. You think he’ll be able to track you down? And would he be crazy enough to come after someone who could legally arrest him?”

There was silence on the line for a moment. “Don’t know. Maybe. Mac, try this. Google me and see if you can ‘find out’ where I live. If you can do it through a regular search engine, then anyone could do it.”

“I will when I get back to the trailer. Uncle Gil had a suggestion. You and Graciella stay out here or at his place,” I told her. “Just for a little while, ’til we can organize a retrieval on this guy.”

Again, silence on the line. “Okay, your trailer is going to be the hardest to find. Let me get some things from my place, and we’ll be out.”

***

I heard the RAV before I saw it. Rosa and Graciella came down the steep switchback to my trailer, taking it slow and careful, as always. When they drove up, I saw the deep dent in the SUV, and it was obvious to a tracker that it was created by both strength and rage. A lot of strength and rage.

Rosa got out of the car, and I was engulfed in a hug as I walked up.

“Sorry I yelled, Mac.”

"Sorry I pushed," I said. "But don't put your life at risk on my account. That's the only thing that's out-of-bounds."

"We'll talk later."

There was an old movie with the tagline "Love Means Never Having to Say You're Sorry." Obviously, the ad agency behind that didn't know their butts from a hole in the ground.

"You know we're going to have to take that guy in, don't you?"

"Yeah. Just don't tell Graci."

"Is she still trying to save him?" I said, disbelieving.

Rosa was noncommittal. "She blames herself for all this."

"Is she going to be mad at you when we take him in?"

She shrugged. "At this point, I don't give a shit."

The problem was, of course, that later on Graciella might find another just like our lover boy. In the meantime, we could make sure there would be one less asshole running free on the planet.

Graciella emerged from the passenger seat of the RAV, and it was all I could do not to wince when I saw her battered face. The area around her left eye was a ghastly eggplant color, and the right side of her lip was swollen badly. It may have been the angle I was seeing her, but her nose didn't look quite centered either. Again, I thought about me and Martinelli, a dark alley and a pair of nunchaku flails.

Gracie knew how she looked. When Rosa introduced us, she kept her head turned as she mumbled "Nice to meet you."

"Well, I'll get my stuff together and you two can make yourselves at home," I said. "I think I'll bunk out here by the river. I like sleeping under the stars."

I didn't mention to Graciella that we were planning on nailing the son of a bitch and collecting the bounty on his sorry ass. She nodded and went to sit down on the deck. The woman was worn out, both physically and emotionally, and Rosa motioned me to follow her down to the little river beach in front of my home out of Graciella's hearing range.

"She's pretty shaken up, still. Mac. You know I don't scare easily, but that apelike psycho running down my car really put ice down my back. Thanks for the idea of staying out here, but I don't think you should go to my apartment, if there's a chance he could find it."

"I googled you, Rosa. It might take him a while, but you're listed in the white pages. That's probably something we should change in our line of work."

"Shoulda gotten rid of my land line years ago," she said. "I only kept it as a line to suck up all the telemarketer calls I get."

"Maybe we should do a little more proactive research on Mr. Martinelli, just to be on the safe side. There may be more to this guy's past than the surface search we did earlier. Either way, we need to get set up with Uncle Gil to do a grab and cuff on this jerk."

Rosa put her arms around me. "I just have a bad feeling about this one, Mac."

"We're professionals. What could go wrong?"

She gave me the eyebrow, and I realized what I'd just said.

Shit.

CHAPTER TEN

***

I need to learn to listen when someone says they have a bad feeling.

I camped out on my little beach, which for me was no hardship. Rosa and Graciella came down after a while to cook hot dogs over the stone fire pit, sitting in the lawn chairs from the deck. Rosa's friend hadn't gained much animation. She still looked frightened and tired. I wanted to ask her about Martinelli, but wasn't sure how to broach the subject, or if I even should at this early date. Luckily, I didn't have to.

"You don't know," she said. "You don't know him. I'm really scared. You don't know what he's capable of."

This seemed like a huge turnaround from earlier when she'd told Rosa to butt out. Maybe she hadn't been thinking of herself at that time, but Rosa.

"Tell me about it," Rosa said to her in a quiet voice. "Share with us."

There was a long silence, Graci staring into the fire, then the words came in a flood.

"It all started out so nice. He made me feel like I was *especial.* He'd buy me things, and say such sweet words… But later on, this all changed. You…he… he can be terrifying. This man, he is frightening all by himself, but he says that he has contacts, that he can find me anywhere. I don't think you have any idea what helping me might lead to. I am weak to have brought you into this Rosa."

"No… it's gonna be okay."

"There is more to David than you think. He is more than just some banger. He said he once worked for the government. Doing bad things, and that he could make someone disappear if he wanted to."

"Could just be tough guy talk," I said, as a chorus of red-alert alarms went off in my head. "You know he's wanted by the law, right?"

She stared into the fire some more. She didn't seem comforted. I got up, went into the trailer and returned with a six pack of beer I'd been saving. She took a cold one from me as if I were throwing her a life ring in the ocean.

"Graci," Rosa said, somewhat tentatively, "we take down men like him and make sure they go back to jail. Let our team help you."

"You have no idea. You said he's wanted for domestic violence and failure to appear. Even if you could take him down, how long would he be in jail for with stuff like that? Probably not very long, and then you know what would happen? He'd not only come for me, but he'd come for you too, Rosa. He likes terror. He loves to make women afraid." For a moment, as she looked up, her expression became determined. "I don't want you any more involved than you already are."

Rosa shrugged her shoulders. "He may be tough, but he's not tougher than my Glock, which I would be glad to introduce him to if needed."

"One thing I'd like to add," I said. "Whether we take him down or not, he would be extremely unlikely to be able to track you out here. My uncle has been working at making me paranoid for half my life. All my records point to my PO box, and if Rosa's here, he's not going to find her either. So, take a deep breath, and relax for a while. You're safe here."

"As safe as possible," Rosa muttered. "He comes after us, he's not gonna be safe."

***

Later, after Rosa and Graciella had gone to sleep in my Airstream, I rolled out my bedroll near the water. The night was clear, so I hadn't set up my tarp. Down here by the river, the dew would be heavy in the morning, but it was summer. My blankets would be dry by 9:00 a.m.

I wasn't really sleeping, at least, not in long stretches. At around 2:00 a.m. I woke again and stared up at the massive star-filled sky above me. I was fairly far from any town, even any streetlights, and the universe spread its incredible jewels before me. It seemed like in a moment like this, one should get some great insight from the Creator of all things, but my mind was in the way.

I'm not sure which thing running around my mind woke me.

As thoughts of Martinelli, or of Johnson, or what Rosa and I had gotten ourselves into bounced through my mind, I lay there, staring at the amazing light show of the Milky Way. Trying to achieve some sort of universal perspective, all I came up with was that we were very small in something very big and our lives were a tiny blip on the face of eternity.

Yeah. Best I could do under the circumstances.

I threw my wool blanket over my shoulders and walked out on the large rock that jutted out into the Columbia River. The magnificence of our galaxy shown back at me from the waters of the deep river, broken on occasion by a ripple from beneath the surface.

I needed to calm my mind. Having my thoughts racing hither and yon almost never brought me anything other than more agitation, so I sat and began to count my breaths. It's the most basic meditation technique there is, and probably the most effective. Being in the dark already, I didn't bother to close my eyes. I just sat as straight as I could and watched the star-filled river roll past. Eventually, the surface of my mind became as smooth as the water.

After I was more in control of my thinking, I began to deconstruct what Graci had said about her "lover" and abuser-in-chief. I'd freely admit he sounded scary.

Anyone who could make Rosa nervous was someone to take seriously. But how much of what he told Graci was real, and how much was bullshit intended to intimidate?

I'm not gonna get this all figured out now. In the morning, it would be best if we did a bit more digging on this man. A simple wants and warrants wasn't enough.

I stood, pulled the wool blanket tighter about my shoulders and turned back toward the shore.

There is something sitting there.

I knew the shape immediately, even though it was just a silhouette. It was a large canine, a coyote. It was the coyote I had seen earlier, many miles and a half mile-wide river away.

It was him. The King.

As if a car had suddenly shone its lights in his eyes, his retinas glowed bright yellow-green and I found myself unable to move, my heart beating rapidly, my limbs frozen.

His face slowly lit, so that for one moment I was looking at King Coyote. And the next, his face changed into the online mugshot of David Martinelli.

I shuddered.

Martinelli's face wavered, and it was the coyote, looking at me intently. Somewhere inside I knew I had been warned. It was not the first time this being, which my part-time mentor Jim Threefeathers told me was one of the Old Powers, had warned me. Those other forewarnings had saved my life.

My limbs suddenly came back to life, and I staggered, dropping to my knees and hunching over for a moment. When I looked up again, I was alone.

I carefully made my way to where the remaining few campfire embers smoldered, using up the last of their warmth. I blew them into flame, adding wood to the fire and sat, pensively, staring into the flames.

I didn't plan on sleeping any more tonight.

***

I did get some sleep, but not until the dawn started to arrive downriver to the east. Rosa nudged me around eight a.m. from where I had fallen asleep in a sitting position, one arm resting on a lawn chair supporting my head.

"Hey, Mister Early Riser," she said. "This is an interesting way to catch your forty winks."

"My neck feels like it's made of concrete and pain."

"Why were you sleeping sitting up like that?"

"I had," I hesitated, "weird dreams. Kinda freaked me out."

"Not… coyote dreams?" she asked.

I nodded. "I think this Martinelli is a lot more than some loser wife beating asshole, Rosa. We need to stay vigilant. I don't know how he'd ever trace us down here, but I can see him finding your apartment. The dream was… creepy."

"I know Gil won't put much stock in dreams, Mac, but I think we'd better tell him everything we know. He's a wily old survivor."

"I think we also might want to see if any of his friends, or Steve Hanger's friends, can find anything more on the guy. I don't think we've dug deep enough."

Bringing up our favorite shadowy soldier of fortune made Rosa pause.

"Really? You think this is 'Steve Hanger serious'? That's not reassuring."

"I don't want you to be reassured, Rosa. I want you to be very on guard 'til we get this guy sorted."

Whatever she was going to say in response was interrupted when my phone chimed from my haversack.

"Hello? Hey, Melinda. How's the search going? Really? Interesting, but hang on a moment," I looked up, "Rosa? Think Graci will be okay here by herself?"

"You wanna go to Gil's then? Let's take her with us."

I nodded. “Melinda? Rosa and I and a guest are coming out. You can show us everything you found. Also, is Uncle Gil there? Would you tell him we’ve got important info for him? Great. Thanks, see you soon.”

“I’ll let Graciella know we’re going. Shall we take the RAV?” Rosa said.

“I know I’m being paranoid, but let’s take the Doom-mobile.”

CHAPTER ELEVEN

***

Melinda was sitting on the porch waiting for us when we drove up. I had barely shut off the engine before she was at my door, obviously eager to share what she'd discovered.

"So I'm guessing you've found something interesting," I said.

"Only where that little shit is from," she told me. "Grew up in Kapaa, middle of Kauai. Found his graduation photo on that site you set me up on."

"Excellent work," I said, handing her all the paperwork she'd given me earlier, along with my notes.

"What's this? Don't you need this anymore?"

"Hope you don't mind, but I made copies of it all, and had it wire bound into a book for easier referencing. It's just a lot easier to manage this way." I opened my messenger bag and showed her the book I had made for the case.

"I'm not worried. Let's go in and I'll show you what I found."

"Sounds good. Hey, is my uncle around? I need to talk to him about something unrelated."

"He and Ed are working on a pump for the well, out back there. They've already seen what I found."

"I can talk to him after you show us."

"So you think you found Jori Johnson?" Rosa asked as we walked into the home office.

"You tell me," Melinda said, a smug look on her face as she pointed to the monitor. There was an electronic facsimile of a yearbook page, zoomed in, and square in the center of the screen was our match. Jori Johnson had only become more of himself as the years went by.

His younger self had the same broad jaw muscles narrowing down to the pointy chin, and the white-blonde hair. There was less wear around the eyes.

There was one thing missing, however. In the other photos we'd looked at, Johnson had a dentally perfect smile, one that would shock your brain into believing whatever gilded lies he told you. The younger version was thinner and closed-mouthed, with a wary, almost haunted look.

"Jordan Brender," Rosa said, reading the name beneath the photo. "A.k.a. Jori Johnson and probably a host of other fake names we don't know about. Well, it's a start."

"More than a start!" Melinda exclaimed. "This is much more than those expensive and useless private investigators ever found!"

"Sure, but let's remember this is just a finger pointing at the moon. We'll still need to research any associates, parents, friends, siblings, what have you, to see if we can get a lead on where this man might be now," I said. "But, you're right. We now have picked up Mr. Jordan Brender's back trail. Have to say though, Melinda, I am very glad to not have to search through all the high schools on the other island. Good job!"

They say that everything in the universe wants to be appreciated, and Melinda reinforced that theory, beaming like I'd put a gold star on her report card.

"So where do we go from here?" she asked.

"Now," Rosa said, "Gilbert has to okay funds for a trip to Kauai, so we can start doin' the bloodhound thing. If we can find one person, anyone, who has kept in touch with this Brender, we might be able to track him to a permanent residence."

"If a guy like this ever uses a permanent residence," I said. "If I'd swindled this many people over the years, you can be sure I'd always be looking over my shoulder."

"You talkin' about Johnson?" Uncle Gil walked in, looking muddy and sweaty.

"Yep. Guess you saw he grew up on Kauai?"

"I did. I'm guessing you want to go there. On the company's dime."

"I don't see how we can move forward if we don't. Rosa and I could…"

"Rosa," he said, looking over his sunglasses, "and you."

"Hey look, I'm not suggesting this so Rosa and I can get a free vacation…"

"But in your spare time, you can just relax a little."

"Fine," I said, throwing up my hands, "this is as far as I can take things from here. You're the big boss, you go to Hawaii, or send Vinnie, or we can just forget the whole goddammed thing."

Melinda looked stricken. "We can't just give up, can we?"

"No," Uncle Gil said, "we can't, Melinda. I made a promise. I keep my promises. I also remember this son of a bitch swindled my sister and I have a personal stake in his comeuppance. I'm just not going to furnish an unchaperoned trip to these two. In other words, all four of us, including Vinnie and myself will go."

"What?" I said.

"That works," Rosa smoothly interjected. "You want me to take care of travel arrangements?"

"Yep. Find us cheap tickets and reasonable lodging." he said. "Let's not bankrupt the company. I gotta go work on that pump some more."

"Hey, I thought I was the search guy," I said.

"You are," he replied, "but I just trust her judgement more." He walked out the door.

"Well," I said. "There it is."

Rosa patted my cheek and headed to the house office.

***

A little later, Rosa and I sought out my uncle and broached the subject of David Martinelli. We brought him up to speed quickly.

"So, you two want to move on this guy before we go then?" he asked.

"It might help pay for this trip," Rosa said. "And it's possible he's coming to us."

"Uncle Gil, I know you don't hold much with the woo-woo stuff, but I know in my gut this guy's gonna be trouble for us one way or another. Might be best if we made that trouble on our terms. He's got bench warrants out, though not for anything that will put him away for too long, but it would at least get him out of circulation."

"Gil, you know I don't scare easy," Rosa said, "but this guy is a chiller. When he was running after my truck, my spine was shivering."

"Sound like it might be a good idea to be proactive, Gil," Ed Burnbaum said from where he was working on the well pump. "Sometimes it's best not to leave a mad dog runnin' the streets."

"All right," my uncle said, "lets get the paperwork going."

"Um, Uncle Gil? You know those hunches I sometimes get?"

"Yeah?"

"We need to dig a little deeper before we go into this. I think you might want to check with your spook contacts. I have a really bad feeling about this guy."

"You want me to call in favors for a wife beater? Mac, c'mon… what has you so het up with this jackass?"

I hated trying to explain this stuff to my uncle, the ultimate skeptic, but it had to be done.

"I… had… a coyote episode."

"Oh for God's sake. Not this mystical shit again."

"Gil," Rosa said, "That coyote saved Mac and me in the Pasayten. It wasn't just him who saw it; I saw it too, and if we hadn't paid attention to its message, we'd both be dead!"

"Coyotes are just animals. They hunt, they eat, they reproduce. They don't get involved in human foolishness, which says a lot about their involuntary wisdom, and they sure don't give mystical warnings."

"Uncle Gil, when you took your guys out on patrol in the sandbox, you told me you always listened to those little hunches," I said. "Ones that sometimes kept your team from getting ambushed."

"Yeah."

"I'm having one of those hunches. We need to get this sorted, or we'll get sorted."

He didn't say a word, perhaps thinking about times when the continuation of his life and the lives of his men was by no means a sure thing.

"Alright. I'll talk to Hanger."

CHAPTER TWELVE

***

I had dropped Rosa off at the trailer and was heading back to Wenatchee to take care of business at the dojo. I was teaching one of the kids' classes each week and tonight was my night. You can talk all sorts of tough guy talk about a martial arts school, but the majority of them are able to survive because parents often like to have their children possess at least a modicum of ability to defend themselves. When they see their offspring becoming more focused and disciplined, well, icing on the cake.

My class had gone well, the usual mix of training with a bit of silliness mixed in. While I tried to keep my young apprentices on track, I didn't make the class into a long discipline-fest. There would be time enough to be dour and straight-faced if they stuck with the martial arts. And I wanted as many to stick with it as I could get.

After I ushered the last of my ducklings out, I locked up. The adult class didn't start until seven that night, and I had an hour to run errands.

I was eating a sandwich down at the riverfront park near a statue of a little boy who obviously loved planes, when my cellphone rang. It was Rosa.

"Hey mister, you downtown?"

"Riverfront park."

"Can I get a favor?"

"You bet. Whatcha need?"

"Undies, socks, makeup, spare ammo."

"Undies and spare ammo, that's my girl. Sure, I'll stop by one of the all-purpose stores. I dunno about makeup though. Anything else?"

"Gabriella had a bag packed, so she's doing pretty good. I have toiletries here, but I could use a couple blouses, another pair of jeans and…"

"Do NOT say Tampax. Do not."

"Tampax. You do have two women staying here now."

"Oh! Guh! Woman! Shall I just mail in my man card now or is there a special drop-off location?"

"You're so sweet. Thank you!"

"Fine," I said with magnanimous resignation.

"Great. Watch for tails when you come home."

"Not my first rodeo, Rosa."

"I know, but better safe than sorry. Love you, bye."

It wasn't that annoying to pick up feminine products, but a guy has to keep up appearances. I could pick up all those things at our local Costco, and bonus points for me, I knew Rosa's pants and blouse size, a side-benefit of buying her Christmas presents last year.

I still had time, so, picking my messenger bag up off the bench, I walked down the river trail. I wanted to take a quick look at Rosa's building, one of the new apartment complexes between the warehouse district and the river. I wanted to see if there were any signs of tampering at her place.

There were a number of vehicles in the parking lot. With the heavy tinting available, it was hard to tell if any of them were occupied, but in the summer heat, I doubted it. None of the cars matched Rosa's description of Martinelli's "piece o' crap low-rider Honda" so I guessed he hadn't been able to find her or hadn't followed up.

Of course, that was no guarantee. Cars weren't that hard to come by on a temporary basis if you knew how to hot-wire them.

I went into the building. Rosa's place on the top floor was pretty nice, if small. It faced the Columbia and had a small balcony overlooking the river trail.

When I got there, the door was slightly ajar.

I should have turned away right then. I should have called the local cops.

Sometimes yours truly is not very bright.

I pushed my way in, slipping my Glock out of my messenger bag's hidden carry pocket. I was barely inside the door when I heard the faintest trace of a sound behind me. I half turned, just in time to see a blurred shape crash into me like a linebacker, taking me completely off my feet.

The impact knocked the wind from my lungs, and my weapon went flying. I smashed into the half-open door, tearing it partly off its hinges.

We hit the floor hard as my assailant had intended and I saw stars. He tried to grab my arms to trap them, but I managed to slam my left elbow into his nose. I felt a satisfying crunch, followed by blood spurting down the front of his shirt.

As far as I could tell, Martinelli wasn't affected by a broken nose in the least, hitting me three times in rapid succession. I blocked the first punch as I tried to get out from under him, but he tangled my free arm. The next two blows hit me in the face like concrete cinder blocks.

I fuzzed out for a moment. When I drifted back, two apelike hands were around my throat. Looking into Martinelli's black eyes, I had no doubt that an insane person was straddling me. It wasn't the repressed fury staring down at me. It was the calm, cool voice that demanded;

"Where's. My. Bitch."

If you've ever tried to form a coherent sentence with someone choking the life out of you, you know my answer was little more than a croak. Martinelli seemed to realize this also, and his hands loosened slightly, giving me a second to pull air into my lungs.

"I want to know where Graciella is, and if I don't hear what I want, I am going to beat the living shit out of you. Do you understand what I am saying to you?" he said in a quiet, intense voice. "I will cripple you."

"You… got the… wrong apartment, nut job."

Martinelli threw himself up slightly from straddling me and drove a knee into my ribs. The pain was shocking, and I was really starting to miss being able to get a full breath of air.

"Wrong answer, dumbass. I'm just going to keep hurting you 'til I get what I want, so do yourself a favor. No need to be crippled for life for that stupid bitch." He pulled back his hand and slammed his fist into my head again. I ducked and took most of it on my forehead, but everything went gray anyway.

"Hey! What are you doing to that man?" I heard someone's voice from far off, and I felt something yank against me. Then Martinelli was off me and I heard a crash, then a woman's scream. A few moments later, an older man appeared at my side, his hand over one side of his face.

"You all right there, son? Oh, no. You do *not* look like you're all right. He pounded you pretty good."

"I've… gnuh…," I mumbled. "He… run off?"

"Yeah, after sucker punching me," he rubbed his face again. "My wife called 911. The cops are on the way. You need an ambulance?"

"Naw. Don't… think so," I said. "My head hurts and I'm a little woozy, but…"

"Honey," he yelled, "make sure they send the ambulance too!"

"No.. I'm…"

"You're probably looking at a concussion, buddy. Not something to screw around with."

"Where's my… bag?"

"He had one as he ran away. Olive drab canvas."

"Mine." I felt in my back pocket and found my wallet

still there. Checking my cargo pants thigh pocket I found my phone, giving me a little peace of mind through the pain. The only thing in the messenger bag had been Melinda's reports, the remains of my food, a small flashlight and my multi-tool. None of those things had my address on them, or even my name. That meant he still didn't know who I was or where I lived. The paperwork might tell him who Melinda was, but he'd have no way of knowing our connection or where she was.

Just then, a Wenatchee police officer walked in and kneeled beside where I was sitting. I knew him and he knew me from our business retrieving fugitives.

"Hello there, Mr. Crow. How are you feeling?" Officer Jim Tanner asked.

"Not so hot."

"Yeah. I can see why."

"I'm Tom Waters," my rescuer told him. "I saw that man beating the hell out of this young fella and tried to intervene. You can see the shiner I got for my troubles. Our friend here might have a concussion."

Tanner seemed unmoved. "Ambulance is on the way. You know who did this, Mr. Crow? One of yours?"

"His name is David Martinelli, from Richland. We helped his girlfriend escape from him. Guy's a psycho. He's already got warrants out for his arrest."

"Well, I think he just bought another." Tanner looked at my battered face for a moment and stepped away to relay the information to his people. I pulled out my phone to call my uncle.

"Uncle Gil? I'm at Rosa's. Martinelli just jacked the hell out of me. What? No, but I'm pretty beat up. Call Rosa, tell her not to come in. WPD is here and they're putting a watch out. I don't want Martinelli finding out where they are. I could… use a little back up here to make sure the mental case isn't keeping watch on me. Yeah, they're taking me to the hospital to make sure I'm okay. See you there."

This was definitely not the way I thought my evening was going to go.

***

"Good pupil response," Dr. Morgan said. "Looks like you have a pretty hard head, Mac."

"Feels like the left side of my face is twice the size it should be."

"Is he going to be all right, Doctor?" my mom asked. She'd been the nurse on duty when I was brought in. "His poor face looks awful!"

"He's pretty bruised up on the left side of his face, but it should go down with some ice. I want to tape up these ribs also. I think they're separated. Give it a week or so, take it easy and the bruising will start to fade. Whoever did this was brutal. You actually got off very lucky."

"If a guy with a face like a stone ape and a very bad attitude comes in with a broken nose, call the cops directly," I said. "He's not someone you even really want to interact with, much less have a problem with."

"Is he all right to go home, Doctor?" Uncle Gil asked.

"Yes, I believe he is, but keep an eye on him, Mr. Chambers. Concussions can be a little tricky, and we don't want any nasty surprises."

"I've already had enough of those today," I said. "Uncle Gil, any word on Martinelli?"

"Cops have a bulletin out for him, Chelan County Sheriffs also. I've got Vinnie roaming the area around here, just in case the son of a bitch might have followed the ambulance. You don't think he got any info from you?"

"My messenger bag had nothing of the sort he could use to find us, and I still have my wallet and phone. I walked down the trail from my truck, and he had no idea I was involved until I went to Rosa's apartment. Unless he's psychic…"

"I'm suddenly takin' this guy a lot more seriously. While you were in here with the doc, I made the call to Steve Hanger. He's having his contacts see if they can find anything deeper and earlier on Martinelli."

"Like I said, I think there's more to him than a basic report covers."

"Yeah. And I'm starting to share that bad feeling you mentioned earlier."

"This just shows that this… bounty hunting business is too dangerous, MacKenzie," Mom told me, looking both scared and angry at the same time.

Oh boy, here we go.

"Yes, it is," I said. "But it is the profession that I have chosen, Mom. Also, this didn't happen because of hunting bounties, it happened because I tried to help someone."

"Also because you were an idiot," Uncle Gil said. "Let's not forget that part."

"Granted," I replied. "I shouldn't have gone there alone. I should have called the cops the moment I saw the door was open."

"Good. You can learn."

"This whole profession of yours is one risk after another," Mom said, voice rising. "You need to find a decent line of work."

"I would like for all of you to stop badgering my patient. Right now," Dr. Morgan interrupted our family feud. "He has a minor concussion, and browbeating him," he looked pointedly at his nurse, aka my mom, "is not helping him in any way. Joanne, take five, and send Anna in, please."

Mom turned to the door but as she left, she looked Uncle Gil in the face and and said, "We are NOT done with this."

CHAPTER THIRTEEN

***

Three days later I was starting to feel antsy, having done my best to follow my doctor's advice. Inactivity is not something I enjoy and the lack of exercise was starting to wear on me.

We all moved to Uncle Gil's place, and I had more nurses than I knew what to do with. Rosa and Graciella hovered over me. Melinda was constantly asking if I needed anything. Mom visited often to badger me about life choices.

I was ready to run for the hills. The treatment was worse than the concussion.

I had gone on a short walk the day before and checked out what the local wildlife was doing through their footprints, but my heart wasn't in it. I really wanted to do something about the guy who had so effectively blindsided me. Having a predator on the loose that had a personal stake in my life was decidedly unsettling.

Unfortunately, Martinelli was not cooperating. Police had seen no sign of the man whatsoever, and Martinelli was a man who stood out in a crowd.

I was sure that I had smashed his nose well enough that he very likely had a raccoon set of black eyes, but no one had even a rumor of his whereabouts.

Steve Hanger, Uncle Gil's friend worked part time for the government as a contractor for 'rough work,' and he had good connections in the intelligence community. Unfortunately, he had not gotten back to us with any background information on my assailant.

"Dude, I got Jessica Walinski watching your truck down in the public parking lot," Vinnie told me. Jessica was a local P.I. who, in our small town was probably thrilled with any kind of work. I had a suspicion that Vinnie was sweet on her and happy to throw something her way.

"Thanks, Vinn, but I think that's just a fishing trip. I can't think of any way that jack-hole could have seen me get out of my truck. I was just like everybody else 'til I opened Rosa's apartment door. He obviously had it under surveillance somehow."

"Sheeze, coulda been anything. He coulda had a webcam in the hallway for all we know. At least you broke his effing nose."

"Small consolation. Didn't even slow him down and my face is still aching."

"We'll get him, don'tcha worry." Vinnie said. "Right now, I'd guess the guy is hiding out somewhere in town. Richland PD said he hasn't been home."

"He's not as stupid as we'd first hoped, that's for sure. Wenatchee's not a big city, and he has a face that only King Kong could love. If he's around here, I bet he'll get nailed eventually."

We were interrupted when Melinda, who had been hovering over me worse than my own mom when she came to visit, stepped out on the porch, a big grin on her face.

"Okay, Mel, what's with your happy face there?"

"Guess who's going to Hawaii."

"Um… who?"

"All of us! Gilbert has decided that everyone involved should get on a plane and go find my swindler," she crowed. "He figures if we're all in Hawaii, you and Rosa and her girlfriend will be out of harm's way."

"How the heck did you get him to sign off on that? Plane tickets and hotel…"

"We won't need a hotel," Vinnie said. "We're staying with a friend of mine over there. He has a fairly large house that we can crash in and use as our base of operations."

"How'd you swing that, Vinn?" I asked.

"Mac," my uncle said, stepping out on the porch and looking at me like I was the slowest student in class, "Vinnie grew up on the islands. How long were you on Kauai, Vinn?"

"From age eight to nineteen. My dad was stationed there," Vinnie said. "My best friend Duke still lives there."

"I had no idea," I said.

"Dude, don't sweat it," Vinnie said. "By the time we leave Kauai, you'll know more about my sordid past than any of us wants."

"Airline tickets?" I asked, hoping to change the subject.

"Rosa found us a good group deal," Uncle Gil said. "First Class for Vinn and me, being owners of this company, and economy for all you plebeian camp followers."

"You're lucky Rosa's not around to hear you call her that."

"I'm no fool," he said.

***

Rosa purchased tickets to fly us out of Wenatchee, not Seattle. While it was an extra hundred bucks each, the extra leg allowed us to arrive less than an hour before takeoff with a five-minute check-in. Doing the same thing at Sea-Tac airport would have taken a good hour or more of standing in lines waiting to check-in, as well as going through Seattle's more involved TSA checkpoints.

The 6:30 a.m. flight over the Cascades to Seattle only takes around thirty minutes, and if you're lucky enough to get a window seat on the turbo-prop Alaska/Horizon Air plane the views are pretty incredible. Being a gentleman, I'd given Rosa the window, and tried to catch glimpses as we flew.

"Mac! Look! Mt. Rainier is starting to catch the sun," Rosa said, looking at the slumbering volcano, its top showing the first light of a new day.

"That's quite a show she's giving us this morning." I said. I looked over at some of my fellow passengers on the opposite side of the plane. They had mountain views equally stunning, and while a few were as entranced as Rosa, most were sitting looking at phones or tablets. I could see doing that on a long flight, in fact I had brought my iPad Mini to binge-watch episodes of my favorite survival show on the six-hour flight across the Pacific Ocean. But on a thirty-minute flight over some of the most gorgeous terrain in the world, I preferred to live in the here and now.

Our time in Seattle was brief, though the airline kept changing our gate, forcing us to take the inter-airport train back and forth. Within the hour, we were making our way onto Alaska Air flight 122. Somehow I wound up in a center seat behind the row containing Rosa, Graciella and Melinda.

I noted that the person in the window seat wore an overstated political slogan on his T-shirt, and it was all I could do to not shake my head. I realized there was going to be a problem when the person sitting beside me in the aisle seat kept glaring at Window Seat Guy.

We were barely an hour into the flight when Aisle Seat couldn't control himself anymore and rose to Window Seat's bait. It started with a snide comment, and for the next hour, I was in the middle of a "debate" which was more snark and insult than reasoned argument.

Both so strongly needed to be right that civility quickly went out the door. I couldn't help but wonder if this was eventually going to be a mirror of our entire nation. Snarkiness on television, snarkiness in political discussion, snarkiness in general conversation.

We'd go to other countries and our reputation would precede us. Our new, even worse, reputation.

I'd had my earbuds in, trying to watch my show on my iPad

until, in their anger, they both leaned in and used my limited space for their argument.

Enough was enough.

"Gentlemen," I said, loud enough for everyone to hear. "It's time to act like grownups, now." This was slightly ironic, as I was twenty-five and both of these "gentlemen" were in their forties.

"Who the hell ya think you are?" Window seat snarled.

"This is a private conversation," Aisle seat growled.

"I'm the person who's had to listen to you both act like little shits for most of this trip. You have both passed the clinical definition of a boor: someone who deprives you of solitude without providing you with company. I have had enough."

The flight attendant had been monitoring the arguments of my two fellow passengers, waiting for them to cross the line but it must have been the look on my face that sent her scurrying over to try to avert disaster.

"Is there a problem here?" she asked. By the intakes of their breath, I knew both of my aisle mates were about to launch into long-winded diatribes, involving myself, their seat opponent, the last three political administrations and possibly the residents of Canada and Mexico.

I stood quickly, exited my row and said, "May I speak with you for a moment? Privately?"

The attendant and I went toward the area between the bathrooms.

"I could see by your face that things were getting heated," she said.

"I've been stuck between those two adult children for over an hour and a half," I replied. "I'm just about on my last nerve. They each have their notion of what's what, and there is no room for any other facts, much less opinions."

"We cannot have passengers threatening and arguing with each other."

"I get that. I have a suggestion for you that is easy, and will defuse the situation all around. I think."

"Let's hear it."

The solution was simple. A few minutes later, Aisle Seat was sitting in the aisle seat, one row ahead. The passenger sitting in that seat, who just happened to be Rosa, was now sitting next to me. Mr. Window Seat was left with no one to talk to, as Rosa and I pretty much ignored anything inflammatory he said.

He sulked the rest of the way to the island.

CHAPTER FOURTEEN

***

Lihue Airport on Kauai is not the hyper-manic place that Seattle-Tacoma is. Like the islands themselves, it moves at its own pace. As we walked out of our plane and into the hallways to baggage claim, my uncle looked around wistfully.

"S'up, Uncle Gil?"

"There used to be beautiful ladies that'd hang a lei around your neck. They'd welcome you to the island. It was a nice touch."

"Maybe we're here on an off day?"

"Or maybe we just flew the wrong airline for that," Vinnie said.

"Maybe. Or maybe someone just decided to cut the hospitality budget," he said with a sigh. "C'mon, baggage claim is down this way."

Our entire entourage trundled to baggage claim and spent ten minutes in front of the wrong carousel until a harried-looking Hawaiian woman in an airport uniform set us straight.

The baggage carousel was surrounded by people I recognized from the plane. I saw a buff-looking dude with an oversized beard wearing sunglasses, jeans and a wide cowboy hat who had been seated a few rows in front of me. He grabbed a couple of huge military duffels and headed toward the door.

Next to the cowboy were the young parents whose baby had cried for half the flight. Rosa told me that babies' ears have trouble clearing the pressure, something that adults take for granted. The kid had a pretty miserable flight, as did the people in the surrounding seats. Now on the ground, she was a little bundle of happy cuteness.

A little ways down, I saw Mr. Window Seat and Mr. Aisle Seat studiously avoiding each other's gaze. I guess even hardcore dogmatists are smart enough to let crap go when they land on the islands.

In the way of Murphy's Law, my bags were the last on the carousel.

"I can't believe we're here!" Melinda said. "I've wanted to go to Hawaii all my life, never could quite bring myself to spend so much money."

"I got us pretty cheap airfare," Rosa said. "Well, except for our two fancy boys." Uncle Gil and Vinnie just looked at each other knowingly.

"It's a lesson," Melinda told us. "I saved like a miser for my retirement, and what do I have to show for it? I should have spent some of that money living while I was young!"

"Hey, Melinda," Rosa said. "we'll find this *pendejo* and get as much of your money back as we can squeeze out of him. Mac's mom's money, too!"

"You're wonderful, dear. Now, could you make me young again, too?"

***

It took us almost an hour to get ourselves out of the airport. We put everyone on the small shuttle to the car rental section and rented a large black van and a smaller sedan. Once done, we took a right out of the airport and headed west.

After stopping at a big-box store so that we didn't show up at our hosts empty-handed we left the commerce center that is Lihue, and continued down the main drag, the Koloa Highway which runs the length of the island.

Vinnie's friend Duke lived in a small town named Hanapepe and without Vinnie riding with us, we might have never found the place. We drove side roads, passing houses with rusting roofs and beat-up cars, along with tiny shops selling tourist trinkets and pineapple.

We turned off on a driveway that went into a forested area and after a couple turns found ourselves at the residence of Duke Kamaka, our host until we could find our charismatic swindler. The house was well kept and looked out over a valley with a flowing river running through it. Large coconut palms surrounded the yard.

As we climbed out of the van, a native man in early middle age stepped out on the porch. Duke was not a tall guy, but he had a big presence. He was kinda thick waisted, but had arms that many weightlifters would envy.

Duke owned his own construction company and he obviously wasn't the kind of man to sit back and watch his employees work. I had the urge to do push-ups before we shook hands.

He strode across the driveway, his face breaking into a big toothy grin. He took the much larger Vinnie into a bear hug and lifted him off the ground.

"Vinnie! Why you take so long to come visit, man?" Duke said, "Hell, my kid's half grown up now. You shouldn't stay such a stranger!"

"Duker! Dude, you are a sight for sore eyes. I been meanin' to get back here, but you know. Business owner an' all that stuff." I heard real regret in Vinnie's voice. Duke must've heard it too.

"Hey bro, you were here when we needed you. S'all good, and now you're here again."

We began to unload, and Vinnie introduced us. It was all pretty perfunctory until Graciella stepped out of the sedan with Rosa and Melinda.

"Well! Hello there! I'm Duke," he said to her. "I… uh…"

"I'm Graciella. I am very pleased to meet you, Duke."

"It's very likewise from here."

"Duke, this is Rosa, one of our team and Melinda," Vinnie told him.

"Ah! The beautiful warrior and the damsel in distress. Thank you both for making this lazy white brother of mine come home for a visit."

"Oh!" Melinda said, surprised. "I didn't realize you two were… brothers? Was someone adopted?"

"In a manner of speaking," Duke said. "Big boy there was once a little boy, one that wanted to surf, and a slightly older boy decided to help him not get hisself wiped out. We sorta became brothers from different mothers."

"Duke and me became pretty much inseparable when we were teens," Vinnie said. "My folks were havin' relationship issues, and I spent a LOT of time at his house. Definitely my second home. Actually, if I think about it, it was more like my first home. It was better than listening to my folks argue and fight all the time."

"You more than made it up, Vinn, holdin' me an' the kid together when… ah…"

"When Marianna died."

"Yeah. S'funny. All these years and I still have trouble sayin' it."

They both grew silent for a moment, lost in thoughts about times gone by and then our host straightened and gestured for the group to go inside.

Duke's place wasn't fancy. Nothing looked new, but it all looked like it was well cared for. A teenage boy sat on the couch, eyes locked with dedication to his phone. Duke frowned when he didn't look up from it.

"That's my son, Mikey…" he started.

"Mike. Just. Mike," The teen interjected.

"Well why don't you get your face outta that phone for a few seconds and say hello to our guests, MIKE."

I'm not sure if it would have been possible to have risen more sullenly. When he did, he turned toward us to say, "Hey."

Then his gaze found Vinnie, and Mike's whole attitude changed. His eyes opened, he stepped forward, and he looked into Vinn's face.

"Vinnie? Holy crap, man! I didn't know it was you comin'!"

"For the love," Duke said, exasperation in his tone, "I told you last week. Why don't you listen?"

Mike ignored his dad. "I'm… glad to see ya, man," he said, almost shyly.

Vinnie hauled the boy into a big bear hug. "Glad to see you too, l'il bro. But Jesus, you're practically a man, now."

"Hey, y'know, it happens." Mike was nonchalant, but obviously enjoyed the praise. "You gonna hit the surf with me? Do some cuttin' on the waves?"

Vinnie, Rosa and I all looked over at Uncle Gil.

"Hey guys, we're got three weeks to find our man. That's enough time to interview half the island," he said. "I'm sure our employer," he gestured at Melinda, "will authorize a few afternoons off."

"So authorized," Melinda said with a wink. "Good labor relations and all that."

***

It didn't take us long to get settled in. Uncle Gil and Vinnie took a guest room, Graciela and Melinda had another empty bedroom, and Rosa had the couch in a little home office area. I was volunteered to a Wal-mart hammock under the coconut trees. Fortunately, the trees had already been harvested, saving me from another possibly lethal bonk on the head.

Once I had my hammock strung and a lightweight silnylon tarp from my wandering bag stretched over it, I went inside where Vinnie, Melinda and Graciella were working on providing us with something that smelled delicious.

"Hey," I said to Rosa, who was sitting in one of the chairs on the porch, "how're your lodgings?"

"As couches go, it's a lot more comfy than some of the places I slept in when I was in the service. How's your hammock?"

"It's kind of a cheapie, but I think if I put a blanket under me as well as over me, I'll be okay."

"Smells like whatever those two are making is getting close to done, want to go in?"

"Sure," I said. "Can't go hunting swindlers on an empty stomach."

CHAPTER FIFTEEN

***

We were all up early the next day. I was up a little earlier because Duke's leaving for work woke me in my hammock. If you've ever been with a group of various early risers, one thing you learn is that you better have coffee ready to preserve the peace.

I had become the de facto coffee maker at my trailer through a series of underhanded maneuvers by the love of my life. She, being Princess Coffeesnob, had told me I needed to get one of the cartridge coffeemakers for my little Airstream. I balked, telling her I was not going to be adding more tiny bits of waste plastic to the world. Having pontificated on the subject for a while, Rosa had conceded the point, either because I was right or because she was tired of my going on about it and wanted her coffee.

The compromise was a medium-priced brewer that I was enlisted to make the coffee in. Part of the deal was that we would not use crummy, bitter coffee. Needless to say, on our shopping trip before coming to Duke's, a can of coffee with an exceptionally fancy-sounding Italian name was purchased. If it has a fancy Italian name, it has to be good.

After properly caffeinating the team, we were ready to interview Brender's former high school classmates. Those we could find.

Uncle Gil and Rosa took the van. Vinnie and I were just getting into the sedan when Melinda came bursting out of the front door, signaling for us to stop.

“I want to come along,” she said. “Maybe I can help.”

“Gonna be a long boring day, unless we get lucky right off,” I told her.

“You never know,” she said. “Sometimes people might open up to a sad old lady before they’ll talk to a pair of gargantuan thugs. Er… no offense.”

Vinnie and I looked at each other, eyebrows raised.

“None taken, Melinda,” Vinnie assured her, “And you’re right, Mac does look like a thug. Sorry buddy, someone had to tell you.”

“My mom likes me,” I said.

“Less so since she had that eye operation….”

I could see how this day was going to go already.

***

Our first stop was a man from the yearbook page of Brender’s high school class, with the name of Morton Glass. In his youth, Glass had looked gawky and scrawny, with a protruding nose and thick-rimmed glasses. I guessed he hadn’t been Big Man on Campus back then, but now he had a nice office in the town of Kapaa selling insurance through a national brand. He’d filled out, got some stylish glasses and a decent haircut and age had been kind. In his mid-forties, his brown hair, thin at the top was only starting to gray. Strange, though. Even living on the island all this time, he still didn’t have a tan.

“So you’re looking for Jordan Brender? Godawmighty, there’s a name I never thought I’d hear again,” he said. “What’s he done?”

“He, uh, pretty much has been tricking old people out of their savings in a phony retirement scam,” I told him. “We’re representing a consortium trying to find him and recoup as much of these folks’ money as possible.”

“In other words, what Jordan hasn’t blown already,” Glass said. “I always knew that kid would turn out to be a criminal of one kind or another. Back in high school, you didn’t dare leave anything valuable unattended if he was near. Damn sticky fingers, if you get my meaning."

"Not surprising," I said.

"So you guys think he's back here, living on Kauai?"

"We can't say for sure," Vinnie told him. We were sitting across a desk from Glass, in chairs that were usually used in the selling of insurance to people with expensive enough things that they needed to join the protection racket that insurance companies peddled. "He mentioned to one of the people he swindled that he missed the islands pretty bad. He could be here, could be on one of the other islands, or he could be on the Caribbean."

"Or in Topeka for all we know at this point. We want to find someone who has kept in touch with him, corresponded, has a phone number for him or any living family members. Right now, we're just trying to pick up his trail. Do you know if his parents or any relatives are here on this island?"

"Sheesh," Glass said, "So long ago. I only know that the family lived somewhere near Kapaa. I do remember that his mother was pretty damn good-looking for someone's mom. And she must've had Jordan young, 'cause honestly, she was hotter than a lot of the girls in our class."

"Any idea where she wound up?"

"Divorced Jordan's old man, traded up. But I have no idea where she is now, or who she married. Sorry."

"How about the father?" Vinnie asked him.

"Phew! There was a piece of work," Glass said. "Professional strength loser. I'll never forget the day the old man came onto our high school campus, three sheets to the wind, and slapped the hell out of Jordan. Took three teachers to pull him off and I think the cops took him away."

"Would I be correct in thinking they weren't close?" I asked.

"You'd be correct, so he's probably not been in touch with

his son in a long time, probably since the mother and the old man were divorced. But, ya never know. Guys and their dads, sometimes even the worst fathers get more chances than they deserve from sons looking for approval. I couldn't say."

"You think either of them is still here?" I pressed for an answer. Chances were good that Jordan might have kept in touch with one of them. Uncle Gil and Rosa were out looking for the mother who could be the harder of the two to track down.

"Couldn't say on his mom, but his dad was the kind of guy that didn't have the kind of gumption or ambition to leave. If he's still alive, I'd bet he's still on Kauai."

"Anything else?" Vinnie asked him.

"I'm sorry guys. I got my first steady girlfriend in my junior year, Hannah, and honestly I kinda checked out from the social scene at high school. That's about all I can tell you about Jordan. There was a kid he hung with, a few grades below us, but for the life of me, I couldn't tell you his name."

"Any ideas on people who might've been more involved with Jordan?"

"Not really. Hannah and I pretty much shut out the world. We're still together today."

"That's better than a lot of people do," I said.

He smiled. "I'm a lucky man."

***

We interviewed two more people on our list. The first, a Mr. Dave Grayburn told us no more than Glass had, and he was obviously impatient to get rid of us. The only reason we got anything out of the guy was that Melinda went into detail about the troubles Brender had caused her.

The second, a Ms. Mary Mateo spent a fair amount of time enlightening us how the Filipino descent population on Kauai and all the other islands was discriminated against because they weren't native Hawaiians. Neither got us closer to Jordan Brender.

Sitting at a little coffee shop in Kapaa, I was using my phone as a hotspot for my iPad. I had Jordan's father's name, Devin Brender, and I was attempting to get into county records to find out if he was currently paying taxes on the last address shown.

Vinnie's phone rang, resounding with some surfin' guitar music. "Hey, Gil." Vinnie said. "Yeah, we're at the Java Kai in Kapaa. Trying to get a lead on Jordan's dad via Internet voodoo. What? Sure. You want us to meet you somewhere? Kauai Beach Villas. Got it. Yeah, I know where it's at. We'll head out."

"All those times I heard surf music come outta that phone," I said, "and now I finally have context. We done here?"

"Gil wants to drop Rosa off so she can come with us. Says he has stuff he needs to do."

"Your ever-cryptic uncle," Melinda said to me.

"Yeah."

"Any luck with the tax search?" Vinnie asked.

"The place that they lived when Jordan was a kid is here in Kapaa, but it was foreclosed on a few years after that yearbook came out. However, there is a place up in the hills currently owned by the father. I can't find that the taxes have been paid there recently, but I can't find that the property has ever been foreclosed on, either."

"Well, let's pick up Señorita Rosinator, and we'll just answer the question with a drive out there."

After a short drive, we found Rosa sitting on a bench out front of the Kauai Beach Villas' lobby, and as she came over to the car, I got in the back seat so she could ride shotgun. There was no sign of my uncle.

"He just dropped you here?" Melinda asked.

"He said he had to run some errands, and wanted me to keep an eye on these two," Rosa said, looking over her shoulder. "You guys have any luck?"

"We may have a lead on Brender's dad," Vinnie told her. "Doesn't sound like they were close, so it may be a dead end."

"That's more than Gil and I got," she replied. "You guys have an address?"

"Have one, it's just a matter of whether he lives there anymore," I said. "And if we can find it. It's out in the boonies."

"Let's go find out."

CHAPTER SIXTEEN

***

After we picked up Rosa, we headed back to Kapaa to see if we could find Jordan Brender's father. Devin Brender's last known residence was toward the mountains up a canyon road, surrounded by open range land. The path kept getting narrower and narrower, leading to a series of gravel, then dirt roads.

The trip up reminded me of our drive to Duke's last night until we came to a small group of various residences that looked like they received little to no maintenance. Sullen people watched us drive by, some white, some native, from under rusty metal roofs and awnings.

"Not the Kauai from the brochures, Vinn," Rosa said. Vinnie just nodded. While we had a general idea where our quarry's father lived, it soon became apparent that finding it was easier said than done.

A man was walking along side the muddy road we were on. Vinnie rolled down the passenger window and called to him.

"Hey man, we're tryin' to find a guy named Devin Brender. You know where his place is, bro?"

He turned and looked at us, no friendliness in his sunken eyes, the skin around them darkened. I was pretty sure from past experiences dealing with people with the same look, that he was quite familiar with whatever his drug of choice was. I just hoped he hadn't damaged his brain to the point of becoming violent. He said nothing.

"I'll give you ten bucks, if you just tell us how to get there," Vinnie said. The man seemed to consider.

"Twenty." The man's voice was surprisingly mellow in tone.

"Damn, you drive a hard bargain." Vinnie handed him a bill. If our would-be informer just decided to start walking again, we were gonna have a problem.

Much to my surprise, the man looked at us and in a cultured British accent, said, "You drive another half mile on this road, until you see a turn off to the left. You'll know which one, because there is an old Peugeot maladroitly sitting on its rusty rims just opposite of the driveway. You quite literally cannot miss it."

Seeing the somewhat surprised looks on our faces, he merely shrugged and started walking up the road again. We drove on.

A few minutes later, we came to the rusty Peugeot, turning left onto a track that made us a bit worried about our rental agreement for the sedan. Deciding to risk it, we powered up the muddy road and after about two hundred yards, we came to an opening in the trees.

Living in an old trailer myself, I don't generally like to negatively comment on people's living accommodations, but there was only one thing to say about Casa Brender. Rosa beat me to it just before the words could come out of my mouth.

"Ai! What a shit hole," she said. Vinnie and I both just nodded.

Being bounty hunters, we'd seen some poorly maintained residences, but this one was a new extreme. The main building, looking like it was made almost exclusively of scrounged rusty sheet metal, sagged at one end as if it couldn't bear to stand up to one more drop of rain. There was an older Ford pickup parked in front that appeared to be held together with rust and bailing wire and it was by far in the best shape of any of the corroding scrap heaps that dotted the yard.

We were far enough toward the mountains that the northerly

rains reached here regularly, and whatever the kudzu-like plants in Kauai were, they provided the only relief from unrelenting ugliness by trying to swallow the mounds of trash around the place.

We simply sat and took in the sights for a moment, hoping the sound of our car laboring up the steep muddy driveway would entice someone to come out and talk with us.

A light rain began the moment we opened the car doors.

"Really?" Vinnie said, looking up. The universe chose not to answer.

"It's warm, we'll be fine, Vinn," Rosa told him.

"I know, but it waited right until we…"

"Someone is out here with us," I interrupted. "Melinda, wait in the car, okay?"

"What do you see, Mac?" Rosa asked.

"Right there, crossing laterally in front of us, tracks heading into the brush. Very fresh tracks." The prints I saw were made only minutes before. I could see crushed grass springing back up and pieces of dirt falling from the ridges at the front of each footprint.

Someone had indeed heard us coming up the drive and had used that opportunity to run for cover.

Both Rosa and Vinnie had entirely new, intense expressions, what could best be called "Serious Game Face." It was the face that said, *be ready.*

I didn't really know the birds of Kauai, but I could tell an alarm call when I heard it. I pointed to an area of brush where a small cardinal-like bird looked down at something from a tree limb. We spread out and moved that way.

"Hello!" I yelled. "We mean you no harm! We're not police, we just want to ask you a few questions about…"

A wild-haired man popped up out of the brush fifteen feet ahead of me. I had the impression of a sickly complexion and very bad teeth before the shotgun came up in front of him.

He fired straight at my chest.

***

The next thing I remember, I heard voices. Angry voices.

"*PENDEJO!* I will fucking kill you!" Kinda sounded like Rosa, but I wasn't sure. I heard several impacts.

"Goddam it, Rosa! You're about to kill him! Stand down!"

"Damn you Vinnie Lugar! Let me go! He shot Mac in the chest with that old shotgun and I am going to…"

"He shot him with rock salt. Look! Mac's moving. Go over there and help him."

There was a moment's silence, nothing but wind in the trees and a gentle rain hitting my face.

Then Rosa, her eyes red and nose running was kneeling over me.

"Baby! Oh, Mac, are you okay?" The fear in her voice was palpable.

"I… ouch! He… shot me. Why'd he shoot me, Rosa?" I was having a very shitty month.

Next thing I knew, I was being smothered against her chest, normally something I relish, but my own chest felt like I'd been hit with a baseball bat.

"Aggh… let me down, can't breathe." She let me go and looked at my chest. Looking down, I saw my two-pocket BDU shirt was torn up at chest level and flecks of blood were seeping through in several points. Rock salt trickled onto the ground and I felt several stinging points under my chin. "Help me up. I need to stretch out my chest."

Melinda had gotten out of the car, probably seeing the whole thing, "Dear God, is Mac all right?"

"It looks like he'll live." Rosa assisted me in getting to my feet, and once there I could see the crazy man on all fours. He was trying to get to his feet and get an arm around his battered ribs at the same time.

"You okay, little bro?" Vinnie asked.

"I'll… get there. What's going on with that guy?"

"He learned not to get on the bad side of an ex-MP, I guess. Rosa kicked his feet out from under him then proceeded to soccer-kick the living shit out of him with her boots. Of the two of you, I think he got the worst by far."

"Can't say I… ngh… feel much sympathy, at the moment." My chest ached, the older bruises on my face ached, and I worried that the fall might have undone the healing on my rib cage.

"He's just lucky we couldn't bring our firearms to the island," Rosa said, giving the man a venomous look. "If I'da had my Glock, I'd have blown his brains out, should he actually have any left from being a meth-head."

"Is he? I only got a brief look at him before the sunuvabitch blasted me."

"Yeah man, he's got all the signs, and we've been smelling some pretty vile chemical smells from the shack there. He's probably makin' the stuff," Vinnie said. "I got no interest in going in and lookin'."

"All right you," Rosa snarled at the man. "Who are you?"

The man, now on his feet but looking none too steady, gave her no response outside of an insolent stare.

"Fine. That's how you want it, hunh?" Rosa began rummaging through some of the junk lying in the yard.

"Rosa, sweetie," Vinnie said. "Whatcha doin'?"

In a voice that sounded like it came from a demon in a horror movie, she snarled, "Lookin' for some rebar, or a nice pipe SO I CAN BEAT HIM TO A BLOODY PULP! MAYBE CRUSH HIS SKULL!"

Rosa had seen I was okay, and I was relatively certain that she was conjuring a version of 'Super Bad Cop' for my assailant. I was also pretty sure it was an act.

Preeetty sure.

Vinnie picked up on it and shook his head sadly.

"Rosa," he said, "they almost put you away for life last

time. Please just…"

"I DON'T CARE! GONNA KILL THAT BASTARD!" She screeched, yanking on a length of pipe protruding from under an old dead VW.

"Aw man," Vinnie said, turning to him, "you had to go and set her off. She's off her meds, you know."

The man tried to move behind Vinnie, his eyes getting larger.

"Hey man, that bi…" he saw the look in my eye, "that woman is crazy! You gotta get her outta here!"

"Mac," Vinnie said, "I knew it was a mistake to get her them Kung Fu lessons." Vinnie fluttered his hands "Oh, it'll help her control her rage! It'll make her a calmer more disciplined person. Yeah. I think we're about to get a demonstration of the folly of THAT strategy!"

"Damn," I said. "Guess you were right on that one. Imagine if she does that spinning kick on his head. Oh Lord, that will be ugly! His skull bouncing down the driveway. Ew!"

"Now, hold the fuck on, you guys," our rube said. "You cain't just come onto my prop'ty and make them threats like that."

"Oh, dude," Vinnie said. "That is SO the wrong attitude to take. If you cooperate a little, we might be able to get her out of this episode without too much violence on your person, but if you keep stonewalling… well, she's probably gonna try to smash down that stone wall, if you get my meaning."

"What the hell do you guys want?"

"First of all who are you? We're looking for a Devin Brender."

The transparent caginess of his expression told me he was going to lie, and he most likely was our quarry. I gave a subtle nod to Rosa, who promptly screamed and smacked the already crack-starred back windshield of the VW, shattering it.

"Jesus!" he said. "All right, I'm Brender! Calm down lady! You all here to arrest me or somethin'?"

“That depends, Devin. Are you doing bad things out here?” Vinnie asked. The cagey look returned and confirmed what we’d already guessed.

“No! I’m just tryin’ to live out here in peace, man.”

“Godamighty, Devin,” I said, “You gotta be… what? In your fifties? Though, whatever you’re makin’ out here makes you look twenty years older. That far along in life, and you’re still this much of a screwup?”

“Don’t talk to me like that, you young punk!” Anger flared behind his eyes. “You’re just a snot-nosed kid. What do you know about livin’ hard?”

“Okay, that’s enough,” Vinnie said. “Just being here and smelling you when the rain stops drizzling is making me tired, so let’s cut to the chase. We’re looking for your kid.”

“Huh?” Brender said, a confused look on his face, “which one? Got five, all with different bitches.”

A slam on the fender of the poor VW returned Brender’s attention to Rosa’s angry face.

“Ixnay on the B-word, idiot,” Vinnie whispered. “She was starting to calm down. Devin, we’re looking for Jordan. We need to find him, to have some words.”

“What makes you think I know where he is? I ain’t seen that little piece o’ shit since his mama left me all them years ago. Damn, that woman was fine. I was her first you know. Thought with a little hard hand, I could keep her under my thumb forever but it was Jordan who ruined that. She wouldn’t abide me… disciplinin’ him. Served me with papers, divorced me.”

“Any idea how we can find your ex?” I asked.

“Dianne? Not really. Not like she kept in touch. One of my buddies said she married some rich shit up ‘round Poipu. Figured she’d be a trophy wife, just thought she’d be mine.” He looked sad for a moment. “Well, whatcha gonna do? Always more tail out there.”

With the gap-toothed, sore ridden, prematurely wrinkled face saying those words, I thought Brender was being very optimistic.

"Do you know if Jordan is on the island?" Vinnie asked.

"No clue. His mama'd likely know. Or that pal of his, Kono? Kona? Native kid he hung out with in high school. Just about as useless as Jordan."

"Got a last name?"

"Ha! That I do remember! Last name's Kalua, like the booze." He snorted. "That kid sure ain't left the island. He was a loser goin' nowhere."

The irony of Devin Brender pointing out that someone else was a loser was powerful, but somehow I restrained myself from pointing it out. Meanwhile, Super Bad Cop Rosa has taken Brender's distraction and used the time to look in through the cracked window of the shack. I could tell just from the expression on her face she'd seen plenty. She pulled out her phone and discretely took a couple of photos. Brender noticed, however.

"Hey! Get away from there!" he screeched. "That ain't your house!"

Rosa, all trace of her earlier act gone, dropped the pipe and walked toward the man. Brender took a step back but Rosa simply bent down and picked up the empty shotgun. She walked over to a steep forested slope filled with brush and flung the weapon as far out into the greenery as possible. It'd take some definite effort to retrieve it.

"Shit! My gun! How'm I supposed to get it now?"

"Do something you're not used to, Brender," Rosa said. "Work at it. Be good to do something besides make meth for a change, wouldn't it?"

"What'd you see?"

"Saw your shitty little lab in there, making misery for others as well as yourself."

"Hey, I been cooperating. You guys don't need to tell the cops."

Rosa leaned in. "Yeah. We do." She began walking through the rain back to the car. "Vinnie? We done here?"

"Yep, in a sec," Vinnie said. "You know your ex's current last name, Devin? Her maiden name?"

"Yeah, an' I'll tell ya if'n you erase them pics she took."

"Deal," Rosa said, surprising the hell out of me. She held out the phone, and Brender watched her erase the photos she had taken.

"You can see that's all of them, now dish out the info or I'll take some more," she told him.

"Okay, okay! Don't know what she goes by now, but her maiden name was Startzel. Dianne Startzel. Seriously though, I been helpin' you guys, can't you just leave it alone?"

"Hmmm. Let me ask my chest," I said. "Nope. My sternum is very upset with you, blasting it with rock salt and all. I'll probably have to mention all this to the cops." I headed for the car. Vinnie followed.

"Have a nice day, Devin," Vinnie called back.

"Fuck you! Assholes. You'll be sorry that…"

We drove down the muddy driveway, missing the rest of his witty retort. Ten minutes later, when we hit cell service, I received a series of delayed texts from Rosa with her photos of Brender's lab attached.

CHAPTER SEVENTEEN

***

Late that afternoon, back at Duke's, Rosa was sending all the info and photos we had from Devin Brender to the Kauai Police Department. Graciella, who evidently had some quality medical training, had helped me make sure all the rock salt was out of my skin and appropriate anti-bacterials and gauze patches applied.

"You are developing a very nice bruise, Mac. Most of your chest area," she said.

"Matches my face, I guess."

"Just about gave me a heart attack," Rosa said. "When I got shot last year, I had my vest on. None of us were expecting to need vests just to go ask some questions today. I automatically assumed he'd killed Mac. He shot him at almost point blank range. It was lucky Vinnie pulled me off Brender Senior."

"I was pretty sure if I didn't, you were gonna kill the guy," Vinnie said after taking a swig of his beer. "Having been the recipient of rock salt from a shotgun before, I knew Mac was gonna survive, and I couldn't have my favorite amazon bein' sent to prison."

"Who shot you?" I asked.

"Henh, me and Duke were trying to sneak onto a beach east of the Poipu area, owned by one of the old cattle families. Ran into one of their hands on an ATV, and the son of a bitch shot first and asked questions later. They take trespassing pretty serious here on the island."

"Sî, I guess," Graciella said. "But it's pretty rough to shoot someone with a shotgun, even one with this rock salt."

"Tell me about it," I muttered. "I'm gonna be sore for a week."

"You're damn lucky you're just sore and bruised," Uncle Gil said from the largest easy chair. "From now on, you three go to any of these back of nowhere places, you better put on your goddammed vests. Capiche?"

"Good advice," Rosa said. "How about down here in civilization?"

"Civilization is a myth," he grumbled. "By the way, Mac, my friend in one of the Three Letter agencies got back to me about your special friend, Martinelli."

"With special friends like that, who needs mugging," I said, "What did you learn?"

"Some trouble in his teen years with violence. Enough that he was looking at going to jail for a while. Was offered an out by the judge to join the army, which as we all recall, was pretty short-staffed there for a while."

"In the sandbox?" Vinnie asked.

"Aiii… just like me," Rosa said.

"The difference between you and Martinelli is that he somehow wound up working with intelligence. Then he just vanishes off the books. No MIA or KIA notices, he just disappears from the records completely."

"Spook," Vinnie said.

"That'd be my guess. A man just up and disappears like that while working for our Uncle Sammie, got to have been recruited. Most likely for nasty business."

"Wet work."

"Yep."

"So, he's some kinda assassin?" I asked.

"Good chance," Uncle Gil said. "Or at least some sort of special operator. Weird thing is that two years ago, he reappeared, no taxes owing, no warrants, and an honorable discharge from the Army. But no fill-in on any details of where he was for eight years."

"Madre de Dios," Graciella quietly said. "Do you think he still has connections?"

"I was only peripherally involved with Intelligence," Uncle Gil said, "doing a little work for the D.O.D., and I've still got contacts enough to find all this out. I owe some favors now, but…"

"Where can I go, where can I hide from such a one," Graciella stood, her voice rising into panic. "How will I ever get my life back if he can track me down?"

"There are ways, Miss Graciella," Uncle Gil said. "Most of them involve new identities and going gray from the U.S. government, but it can be done. You might also be harder to track down in Mexico. I asked my contact to relay that this guy is most likely using his government access to information for private matters that entail abuse of power. If he pisses off some high-ups, that could red-flag him."

"I had a life," she said, her face starting to turn to despair. "It wasn't such a bad life."

"Hey lady," Duke said, from a wicker chair where he'd been listening to us. "You stay here with me on the island. We'll change your name to Keiani, and that white boy'll nevah find ya. Us brown skinned folks all look the same to white people."

"Asshole," Vinnie said. Grinning, Duke scratched his head, pointedly using only his middle finger.

"Maybe I'll take you up on that," she said.

"It's an open invitation."

"So," Vinnie said, "tomorrow. What's the plan?"

My uncle looked at me. "I think tomorrow, we'll take a day of rest. We're here long enough that we don't need to be on this every minute. My nephew is probably not in the best shape, at the moment, and maybe a day at the beach might help him heal up quicker."

There was dead silence, the entire group staring open mouthed at Uncle Gil.

"Okay who are you, and what have you done with my uncle?" I said.

"Fine assholes," he said. "Everyone can get up at five a.m., and we'll start…"

"No, no, no, Gilbert!" Rosa interceded. "No take backs! Someone promised me they'd teach me to snorkel while we were here, and I intend to hold him to it."

"But what about Melinda and Mom's money?" I said. "Jordan could be spending it, right now."

"He could," Rosa said, "but you need a rest after today, and we're going to take a day off."

And that was that.

***

Early (but not too early) the next morning, Rosa, Melinda, Vinnie and I headed for Poipu beach. Duke had the day off, inviting Graciella to a picnic at the north end of the island, pointedly not extending that invitation to anyone else. No one was offended.

We found ourselves at Nukumoi Surf Co., across from Poipu Beach, and a very useful gentleman helped us find fins, masks and snorkels. The cultured lady behind the counter was the owner, and wished us a delightful swim. Walking across the street to the beach, Rosa went into one of the changing restrooms while the rest of us waited.

"Don't know why she couldn't just wear her swimsuit like the rest of us," I said. I looked toward the beach, trying to decide which of the sections might be best to teach a beginner how to snorkel.

"Oh my. Dude, I think I have your answer. Turn around," Vinnie said.

Turning, I saw Rosa come out of the women's room in

a truly skimpy white bikini that I had never seen before. It covered everything that modesty demanded, but did so in very daring ways. Melinda was kind enough to reach up under my chin and close my mouth for me.

Rosa looked at me knowingly, and did a spin for me.

"You likey, Mistuh?" she asked.

"Um… uh.. Wow…"

"I think the verbal centers in his brain may have overloaded, dear," Melinda said. "Let's point him toward the beach and give him a little push."

"Y-you look incredible, Rosa," I said. "You look… great!"

"Why thank you, good sir," she said, drowning me in a hundred-megawatt smile. She walked by me toward the beach, nudging me with one mostly bare hip and I followed.

"Uh, dude," Vinnie said. "Snorkel gear."

"Oh, right."

Rosa cut a swath on the way to the sand. Every heterosexual male in the area turned to look as she went by, as did every woman. The looks on the men's faces were universally pleased, looks on the women's faces were a rather mixed bag.

What made the contrast between Rosa and most beach dwellers wasn't just the fact she was so stunning. What you might consider normally shaped people were in a definite minority. With the advent of a sugary coffee shop on every corner in America, and the embracing of Wine Culture and Fast Food Culture, seventy-five percent of the people on the beach were carrying at least an extra twenty-five pounds, many of them much more. Anyone in shape stood out like a sore thumb.

And Rosa was in very good shape.

Melinda set up her chair and went to wade in the shallow sandy section. Vinnie struck up a conversation with a female lifeguard.

Rosa and I, having left our bags by Melinda's chair, took our snorkel gear to the beach between two points. I checked her mask, making sure she had a good seal, then ran through how to clear her snorkel and put on her fins. When she was ready, I put on my own mask and helped her walk backwards into the surf, carrying my fins.

Rosa was already an okay swimmer, so once she was deep enough to swim, I turned her loose and slipped on my fins while I floated. I was wearing a T-shirt to cover my bruised and banged chest, but when I hit the salt water with that area, the stinging was impressive for a few moments. But like the old saying goes, you can get used to anything.

We stayed close to shore for a while. Once she lost her mouthpiece and got a little panicky. I kept her afloat by holding on to her and kicking mightily with my fins until she got it back in place. With her wearing that swim suit, I didn't really mind helping out.

A red-headed woman wearing a shorty wetsuit had a tube of fish food, and splashed a little our way as she swam past. A moment later, we were swarmed as colorful fish of all kinds, some tiny, some almost as big as my thigh, dashed around between us.

I could see through the distortion of Rosa's mask that she was like a kid at Christmastime. If I could have grinned with the snorkel in my mouth, I would have. The mercenary fish soon followed the wetsuit lady.

We swam until we were half-stupid with fatigue, then headed back to shore. As we emerged and took off our gear, Vinnie and Melinda met us.

"Mac, Rosa," Melinda said. "The police called Rosa's phone about five minutes ago and asked where we were. I told them and they said not to leave, that they were sending someone out to talk to you."

"More info on Mister Meth Maker you think?" Rosa asked.

"Don't see what else it could be." Vinnie replied.

"I'm gonna dash to the changing room. This isn't the outfit I want to be questioned by the cops in."

"Mac and I'll be over by the parking lot," Vinnie told her. She waved and took her things with her. "Melinda, why don't you hang back and watch us from over there," He pointed to a grassy area about fifty yards from the lot. "I'd prefer that you not be involved with the police unless there's some reason to be."

"You and me both, mister." She said. Melinda took up our gear and walked away, making sure she could watch us from her position.

As Vinnie and I walked to the lot, he said, "Geez. I hope we're not gonna be called upon to testify in court, man."

"It was pretty obvious as to what he was doing. Probably just an affidavit and our photos would cover it I'd think."

"Hey. Cruiser," Vinnie said, pointing to a KPD vehicle that was pulling into the lot. We waved, and the car stopped in front of us. Two officers got out, both of them native, both thick and strong looking with close-cropped hair and expressions that gave nothing away.

"I'm Officer Kama. This is Office Hale."

"I'm Vinnie Lugar. This is MacKenzie Crow."

"We received a call from a Ms. Fernandez, is she here?"

"Here, I am." Rosa came trotting up, now clad in shorts, sandals and a red blouse. Officer Kama nodded.

"Thank you all for being cooperative. We need for you to come with us in the cruiser back to our station in Lihue for questioning." He gestured toward the police car.

"Was there some problem with the information we gave?" Vinnie asked.

"You might say that," Officer Hale said, peering at us over the top of his mirrored glasses.

"The fellow you said was making meth, Devin Brender," Kama said.

"Yeah?"

"He's dead."

CHAPTER EIGHTEEN

***

"So let me get this straight. The three of you are… bounty hunters?"

Detective Jeff Smith stared at Vinnie, Rosa and myself across a standard table, one like you might find in police stations in any state. He'd seen all our IDs, carefully sorting through each without answering any of our questions. His partner, Detective Nakamura, leaned against the wall and stared at us impassively.

"Yes, Detective. Like it says there on our IDs," Rosa told him.

"You bring any firearms on the island?"

"We're familiar with Hawaii's firearm laws," Vinnie said. "We didn't bring any."

"Can't you please tell us what this is about?" I asked. "All we did was report that Brender was making meth, which if you've been up there must've been pretty obvious."

"Actually, mister…" he looked at my ID, "Crow, it was less obvious than you might think, though we did come to that conclusion eventually."

"I looked into his window. It was right out in plain sight," Rosa said. "He managed to hide it?"

"Not exactly, it just took us a while since everything was burned in the explosion. Including Mister Brender."

"Explosion?" Vinnie asked. "He got careless with his chems or something?"

"Maybe. I understand he shot one of you? With rock salt?"

I lifted my T-shirt, Smith whistled.

"Damn, son. That is a hell of a bruise you got there."

"Yes. Yes it is."

"Piss you off pretty bad?"

"What you mean is, did it piss me off so much that I'd murder Mr. Brender, then burn his house down around him to hide the fact, don't you? Then of course, as any villain would do, I would've instantly called the cops so that they could go there and examine my nefarious handiwork?" I said, perhaps a little more snottily than I intended. "Really?"

"Well, now that you mention it…"

"Then let me make this my official statement, sir," I said, trying to sound as professional as possible. "Around two thirty yesterday afternoon, my colleagues here and I drove up to Mr. Brender's home, such as it was, and got out of our car in the rain. We are seeking information on the man's son, one Jordan Brender, who is wanted under a number of aliases for bilking older people out of their retirement savings. He's scammed quite a bit out of a number of senior citizens, leaving them destitute in many cases."

"I hate guys like that," Nakamura chimed in. "One screwed over my mom and…" Seeing Smith's look, he stopped and said, "Go on, Mister Crow."

"We're here trying to get some justice, and hopefully some cash back for those people," Rosa said. "Go on Mac, tell them what happened."

"As we approached the house, I saw fresh footprints leading into the brush. I followed the prints--"

"How could you tell they were fresh?" Smith asked.

"It's his thing, Detective. Does tracking for our local sheriff departments sometimes," Vinnie told him.

Smith looked at me, eyebrow raised.

"I've got references," I said. "The three of us have also worked as temp deputies to help out an understaffed department."

"Interesting," Smith said, "but please go on with your statement."

"I approached the brush, Brender popped up with his shotgun and let me have it. Things get a little hazy for a bit after that."

"Rosa here disarmed Brender," Vinnie said. "She got Mac to his feet and we interrogated the guy. We got a few leads, and while I talked to Brender, Rosa looked in through his windows and saw the meth lab. She sent you guys the photos when we got home."

Smith looked at Rosa with new respect. "You disarmed him?"

"Yessir. Ex-marine," she said. "MP."

Smith rolled up a sleeve. Under it was a tattoo of a familiar anchor and globe. "Semper Fi, Marine. You go to the sandbox?"

"Ar Ramadi," She said.

"Ah. Fallujah for me." He rolled down his sleeve. "You too?" he asked Vinnie.

"Naw. Army here."

"I won't hold it against you."

I couldn't help but notice he didn't ask me, though I was technically old enough.

"So, when you disarmed this fella," Smith asked Rosa. "How enthusiastic were you?"

"I may have bruised him some," Rosa replied. "But when we left, he was standing in his driveway, glaring and swearing at us because he knew we were going to turn him in for the meth. By the way, his shotgun was flung down into the brush somewhere."

"All right," Smith said. "It's likely that Mr. Brender burned his own roast, but the timing was strange. Will you all be here on the island for a while?"

"A couple more weeks," I said.

"Give me all your phone numbers. We'll get in touch if we need to talk to you again. But rest assured, I am not 100 percent convinced that you three had nothing to do with the man's death. Expect that I will be watching you."

***

Melinda picked us up, and we all had a late lunch at *Rock and Roll Sushi* in Poipu. Situated in a small marketplace with tourist shops, the restaurant was also a prime nesting spot for the island's wild chicken population. One bold rooster eyed me as I ate, either wanting to see if something I had was tasty, or if I might make a savory nugget myself.

"Well," Rosa said, "That was damn odd timing, for ol' Devin to screw up and check out."

"No great loss to the world," Vinnie said.

"Vincent!" Melinda scolded. "As long as a person is in this world, they have a chance to redeem themselves. You shouldn't talk that way about another human being, even if he was a pustule on the ass of the humanity."

Vinnie looked at her, unsure if she was yanking his chain or if she was serious.

"Well, Mel," he finally said. "I just really doubt he was ever going to give redemption a shot."

"He was a pusher of drugs, hooking people on something so addictive and destructive that most never escape its clutches until it kills them. I have NO sympathy for that man," Rosa said with such vehemence, that we all looked at her a little surprised. "Such a person hooked my own mother on heroin, ruined her life and almost ruined that of my brother and sister as well. If I hadn't dragged them out of there and called Tia Maria to come get us, I don't even know what would have happened."

She got up abruptly and walked out of the restaurant. We all watched her a moment, then Melinda nudged me.

"Go after her," she said.

"This seems like something pretty private. She's never been willing to talk about her past with me…"

"Then go make the effort again. Some walls have to be chipped at again and again, and if she doesn't want to talk about it, at least she'll know you care enough to try."

"Mel's right, dude," Vinnie said. "No points for sittin' on the sidelines."

They were right. I stood and followed Rosa. Outside the restaurant, it took me a minute or two to locate her. She was sitting in the center area, a small amphitheater of concrete and stone, watching a hen that was hunting for any fallen food that might have made its way to the ground. She glanced up as I walked over, then quickly looked back at her feet.

"Hey," I said, leading off with my very best in witty openings.

"Hey," she said, barely audible.

"Just thought I'd come see if you were okay."

"Yeah," she nodded. "I'm okay. Sorry I stormed out. Wasn't anything any of you said."

"No one was offended. Just worried about you. Rosa," I said, reaching out and gently tilting her head up so I could see her eyes. They were starting to fill with tears. "If you ever want to talk about any of that stuff, I'm here to listen, not judge."

She reached over and took me into her arms, putting her forehead against my throat. She let out a ragged exhalation.

"Maybe… someday."

"Like Duke told Graci, it's an open invitation."

We sat in the warm Hawaiian sun for a while, as the hen began rounding up an astonishing number of chicks.

"Hey Rosa, you know what you said about damn odd timing?"

"Yeah. Old Man Brender's probably been making that shit for years, and he blows himself up the minute we leave, or close thereabouts."

"Yeah. I don't like it. I got no proof, but I have a bad feeling 'bout this."

"Regular bad feeling? Or Obi Wan bad feeling?"

"Definitely a little in the woo-woo range," I said. "I close my eyes, think about Devin, and I just get this bad feeling in my gut."

"We didn't kill him."

"Then who did?"

"Maybe it was coincidence. Maybe he did it to himself, Mac."

"Maybe. Just wish my gut would unclench."

CHAPTER NINETEEN

***

That evening, it was Duke who helped us with a lead. We'd all been sitting around out on the deck, listening to the Rose-Ringed Parakeets returning from the mountains in the waning sunset light. They settled into their coconut palm roosts, and conversation became easier as their calls lessened.

"So, the cops let us go," I told Uncle Gil. "They didn't have any reason to hold us, but Smith wasn't totally convinced we had nothing to do with it."

"Sounds like Brender's father was a train wreck. Melinda, Graciella and I'll go to Poipu and see if we can trace his mother, while you three go and find this Kona or Kono Kalua person," he said. "I can probably trace the mom through records, but I haven't found anyone with the friend's name in the phone records."

"Ten to one the meth head remembered the kid's name wrong," Duke said. He and Graciella had returned from their picnic, and I don't think it was my imagination that they definitely seemed on friendlier terms.

"Let's also remember that by now, this 'kid' is Jordan Brender's age, late thirties," I said. "I guess we can check out everyone named Kalua on the island until we get lucky."

"I know someone you could hire. Might make the search go faster," Duke said, nonchalantly checking his fingernails.

"Do tell," Uncle Gil said. "Who might that be?"

"The Skateboard Kid," Duke pointed toward his son, who was sitting against the base of the couch near Vinnie, looking at his phone. Uncle Gil raised an eyebrow.

"Vinnie," Duke said, "You know what the skate-surf rat community is like. Mikey, though you wouldn't guess it, likes to do both. When he's not on that damn phone that is."

"Dude, you think you could help us out?"

"How much you gonna pay me, bro?" Mikey asked.

"Ow, Mikers! That's harsh. You could just--"

"It's not harsh, Vinn," My uncle interrupted. "I respect a young man who realizes his time here on Earth is worth something."

Mikey inflated a little at the word respect.

"You think you can provide us with some useful help?" Gil asked.

"I don't, you don't have ta pay me. I do, and you pay me all my hours worked."

"You can't say fairer than that, Mike. So, hourly. How much per hour?"

"Twenty-five."

Uncle Gil laughed. "I'll pay you ten an hour."

"Twenty."

"You drive a hard bargain, son. Fifteen. My final offer."

"Cash? Under the table?"

"If that's what you want."

Mike stood up, walked over to my uncle who was trying not to grin, and stuck out his hand. "You got a deal, Mr. Chambers."

"Mikey'll do a good job for ya, Gil. He knows a lot o' people and those people know a lot of people. You'll find this guy."

"You prefer Mike, don't you, son?" Uncle Gil asked, shaking his hand.

"Yes, I'd be real happy if you'd not call me Mikey."

"I like to keep my employees happy."

"What!? When?" Rosa and I chimed at the same time.

"Within reason, of course," Uncle Gil said, smiling.

***

We started in Kapaa the next day, where Jordan Brender had grown up, and the most likely place to start our search for Brender's friend. Assuming that Devin Brender had a clue about the potential of his son's friend to move up in life, it seemed a better bet than trying to start in one of the other villages along the Koloa Highway.

This of course assumed that Brender senior hadn't been completely full of crap. A big assumption.

The day was tedious, but Duke had been right. Mike was definitely able to get the locals to open up to us more than we could have on our own.

We canvassed the area, looking for former classmates. I was glad I'd spent more time on the computer as I'd found a few addresses which were good leads. Locating these people from a twenty-year-old yearbook wasn't all that easy. When the recession hit Kauai, jobs got tight, and people moved to the mainland looking for work.

Using the on-line yellow pages, we managed to find a few. Most of them barely remembered Jordan Brender, until we quoted Morton Glass about Brender's light-fingered ways.

This did indeed spark a few memories. Our primary accomplishment, however, was confirming the name of Jordan's side kick: Joseph Kana Kalua. A quick return to the phone records, and we had an address. Oddly enough, Mr. Kalua had a business of his own, putting the lie to Devin Brender's evaluation of Kalua as a loser.

"Wave Master Tours. Out of Hanalei, north end of the island," I told Vinnie and Rosa.

"I can get you a lot more info on that business," Mikey said. "If you pay for lunch."

"Geez, Mikers, how much you gonna squeeze us for?" Vinnie asked.

Mike's smile was huge. "I dunno, whatever the market will bear."

"I forgot that feeding a teenager was a full-time job, dude. Tell you what, lets go to the Coconut Market, there's that little stand there in the middle that makes a good burger."

For a moment, Mike looked stricken and started to raise a hand, but Vinnie kept talking.

"Hey! We could go to Eggbert's! I know it's almost noon, but I wouldn't mind some of their banana pancakes, eh dude?"

Mike shook his head, but didn't say anything.

We drove south on the Koloa Highway to the end of Kapaa, and turned into a complex with a sign that said Coconut Market, which promised dining, shopping and events. As we pulled into the parking lot, there was a farmer's market set up across the west end and locals were selling a wide variety of produce. Vinnie almost sprang out of the van, with an enthusiasm he usually didn't show.

Mike looked at me, then at Vinnie, and shook his head.

"What's up, Mike?" I asked him quietly.

"Vinn-Man's gonna be disappointed."

Following Vinnie though a breezeway into a central courtyard, we saw what looked like store fronts surrounding the entire inner area. Most of them were boarded up. A few were open, most of these being from the semi-chain stores we'd been seeing all over Kauai, and these looked to be selling very little of their trinkets and T-shirts.

"Where's the little hamburger place?" Rosa asked Vinnie.

"It… it should be right here," he said, gesturing to a stall with a few plastic lawn chairs under its roof. There was construction paraphernalia all over the complex and obviously some sort of renovation was going on.

"Looks like it's gone," I said.

"Eggbert's?" Vinnie asked. Again, Mike shook his

head. “Aw, man, Mikers, how could Eggbert’s not be here anymore?”

“I dunno, during the recession, buncha people hit hard times, and I heard the owners of this place wouldn’t give no one a break. Here’s the result.”

We wound up eating at the remaining small pizzeria in the complex. Vinnie barely touched his, but he did buy us all lunch. As we headed for the car, Vinnie kept apologizing to Rosa and me, regretting pulling us along on his hunt for the mythical Eggbert’s. We assured him it wasn’t his fault. Bad management is bad management.

Mike left us for a few minutes, going into one of the trinket shops and emerging with a couple of pamphlets.

“Here ya go, more information. A deal’s a deal.” He handed me two slickly produced brochures covered with bikini clad girls and every form of water sport Kauai offered. The slickly designed logo across the top said WAVE MASTERS.

“I think we’ve been had,” Rosa said.

***

The drive up the main highway to Hanalei didn’t take that long, but the scenery made us want to take the trip slowly. Driving from west of Poipu, heading east and north the island changed from open rangeland filled with short trees and cacti, to a lush tropical forest with gigantic mountains rising from the mist in the background.

Mike’s brochures actually were useful. Aside from information on all the different activities that the company provided, the back of one had a brief narrative about the owner of the company, one Joseph Kalua. He was a self-made man, having started with nothing but a Zodiac raft and some snorkel gear for the tourists. His business had come a long way since then. I hoped to heck this was the guy we wanted to talk to, because he was a far cry from the loser that Devin Brender had described.

"We should call ahead," Rosa said, looking up from the other brochure.

"That usually ain't the way we do things in this biz, as you well know, Ms. Fernandez," Vinnie said.

"Kalua isn't a felon, so asking politely would be in our best interests. Also, the guy may live in Hanalei, but Wave Masters main office is in Port Allen. My guess is the Hanalei address is just a mail drop."

Vinnie and I looked at each other. Rosa was right. Again.

We pulled over, and Vinnie got out his cellphone. Rosa, Mike and I exited the van to stretch our legs and look at the lush greenery. There was a stand nearby selling fresh coconut milk and we went over to sample their wares.

"Hey, look!" Rosa said, pointing to a dent in the side-road we'd parked by. "Look in this pothole, Mac."

I walked over and saw the hole had been filled entirely with coconut husks. When I looked up into the face of the older woman who'd been behind the stand. She grinned.

"Best to use what you got," she said, pointing to a number of potholes filled with husks. "Beddah for the environment, and besides, it beats waiting for government to get their butts out here. You kids want some coconut milk?"

"Sî! I mean, yes ma'am!" Rosa said. "Always eager to try something new."

"Sure," I said. "Let's give it a shot."

"None for me, thanks," Mike said.

The vendor took out a small Rambo-style machete, and with a few whacks had opened the tops of two coconuts. She stuck paper straws in each and handed them over after I paid her. Walking back to the van, I quickly filed raw coconut milk/water under *survival only* foods. It wasn't bad, mind you, but it didn't taste particularly good either. I now knew why Mike had passed. The good thing was, when done I could toss the container, an empty shell into the brush without feeling like a litterer.

Vinnie was sitting waiting for us. "Good call." He pointed his finger, pistol-style, at Rosa. "I got his wife or lady friend or whatever, and after finally convincing her I wasn't one of the very tardy landscapers, she confirmed he's in Port Allen. Weird thing, though. I called Wave Masters, and it went to voicemail. You'd think with a supposedly booming business like that, someone could pick up the phone."

"Could've just been an overwhelming flood of calls," I said.

"Maybe," Rosa said. "Let's head down there and see for ourselves,"

CHAPTER TWENTY

***

It's almost always a bad sign for police cars, lights flashing, to be parked outside of the building of the contact you're going to see.

We pulled up and watched from a distance. Officers were scrambling around the storefront for Wave Masters and shortly thereafter, a stretcher came out carrying what could only be a body under a sheet. An ambulance whisked it away toward the highway.

"Look," Rosa said, "Detective Smith."

"He doesn't look pleased," I said.

Vinnie, to our surprise, got out of the van.

"Vinnie, we're not really involved here. We probably don't want to be." Rosa said.

"If that's Kalua under that blanket, then I think we do. Our two main sources of info, both suddenly D.O.A.? That doesn't sound like a coincidence to me. You call Gil. Let him know what's happening."

Rosa pulled out her cell and made the call while Vinnie and I started over to talk to the detective. He was surprised to see us, and suspicion instantly took over his expression.

"Well. Look who's here. Very auspicious timing gentlemen," he said. "Actually, I mean suspicious timing."

"Was that Joseph Kalua under the sheet?" Vinnie asked.

"It was. And I assume you two and he were in some way connected?"

"We were on our way here to interview him. He was, at

one time, best friends with the guy we're trying to find. We've never actually spoken to him."

"Well, someone sure spoke to him. The girl who runs the main desk went to lunch, leaving Kalua in charge of the office. When she got back, the office was closed and when she went inside, she found her employer, duct taped to a chair and dead as my dreams of retiring rich." Smith paused for effect. "He'd been beaten severely, and his neck was snapped. The girl had to be given a sedative to even tell us what happened, she was so hysterical. It was ugly."

"This can't be a coincidence," I said.

"Ya think?" Smith said, looking at me in what could only be described as an accusing manner.

"Wait a second. We had nothing to do with this man's death, or, as we said before, that of Brender's father!"

"Really? 'Cause right now, you two are my most solid leads on two murders, both of which happened after you people landed on the island."

"Officer?" a young voice said from behind me, "There's no way Mac and Vinnie coulda killed that guy."

"Mike, you were supposed to wait in the car," Vinnie said.

"Think about it Vinn," Mike said. "If he was killed at lunch time, we were in Kapaa, at the pizza place. You even paid with your credit card. Forty-five minutes ago, Mac, Rosa and I were getting coconut milk from the lady on the way to Hanalei and I'm pretty sure she'd remember us."

"Who's this? You seem to be recruiting your accomplices pretty young." Smith looked at Vinnie and me. "So. Alibis."

"He's not lying, Detective. We can confirm on both of those," Vinnie said. "We only just learned Kalua's identity and business this morning. We have no reason to want him dead."

"Quite the opposite," I said. "He was our best lead to our swindler."

A police detective never wears a more sour look than when he loses his prime suspects. We had come waltzing up the scene of the crime, vaguely involved with another murder the day before, and it was like a gift. Now, through facts, we had cruelly taken his easy collar away. We were indeed bastards.

"Then do you have any idea who might want these two men dead? Because I am sure these murders are related, and you two and the marine over there are the only connection I see."

"Well, sir," Vinnie said. "If I was to speculate, it seems like the one to benefit from their deaths would be Jordan Brender himself, though how he'd know we're after him, I have no idea."

"If that were true, it would mean he IS on Kauai," I said. "Hell of a way to flush him out though."

"Swindlers don't usually turn to murder," the detective said, "Seems flimsy to me."

"I can't think of anyone else who'd have a reason to shut them up," I said. "Gil Chambers, our employer, is trying to locate Brender's mom. I hope to God that he wouldn't do this to his own mother."

***

It was a quiet ride back to Poipu.

It hadn't taken long for Smith to confirm our alibis, much to his further disgruntlement. The credit card record was clear, but such things can be finagled. The clincher was the coconut lady. An officer went to her stand, and showed her photos that Smith had taken with his phone. Thank God, Pele, or the universe, she had remembered us.

Rosa, Vinnie and I were mulling the probability that Jordan Brender had somehow seen us coming and had started killing anyone who could lead us to him. Truth of the matter was, it did seem unlikely. We were all racking our brains as to how our security might have been compromised.

"I don't see how he could have known," Rosa said. "It just doesn't make sense."

"Maybe Devin Brender knew more about his son than he let on," I said. "Called ol' Jordan up and said come on out, we need to talk about these law-dogs askin' questions."

"I dunno," Vinnie said. "Sounds like poundin' a round peg into a square hole."

"I never seen a dead guy before," Mike said from the back seat. The honest truth was that he still hadn't, not really. Just a shape under a sheet, but we were acutely aware that we'd taken a fourteen year-old all too close to a murder scene.

"You gonna be okay, Mikers?" Vinnie asked.

"Yeah, I'm okay, it's just… y'know."

"Creepy? An awful way to go?"

"Yeah. I mean that guy has… had a life, some lady is waiting for him at home. What if he had kids?" Mike looked out the window. "You start thinking about dying someday, too."

"Every moment's a gift, buddy. Don't waste 'em."

"Good advice," Rosa said.

"Yeah. I guess so," Mike said, but I could see he was deep in thought on the subject.

***

We met Uncle Gil in Poipu, offering to drop Mike off at his house on the way. He'd wanted to stick with us. We pulled into the small market place and walked to the Surf Taco shop where Melinda and my uncle were eating.

"I'm glad I don't have to go and collect you four from the local hoosegow," Uncle Gil led off.

"You can thank Mike here for that," Rosa said. "I think he's earned his pay for the week." Mike blushed, but I could see he liked the praise. "If he hadn't told the detective about our alibis all the while looking at him with those big brown eyes…"

"Good job, son," Uncle Gil said. "So, it appears we're being watched. Impressive bit of surveillance for Brender to carry off. I wouldn't have thought a swindler could be so ruthless cleaning up his backtrail."

"Well," Rosa said, "stakes are pretty high for him now. I guess the loss of his estranged father and childhood best friend were worth not being found."

"If it is Jordan behind this," I said. "We're guessing here."

"Dear God," Melinda said, looking suddenly aghast. "I brought us all into this. I'm partly to blame for those men's deaths."

"That's bullshit, Mel," Uncle Gil said. "Our being here might be a catalyst, sure. But we didn't tell anyone to start a killing spree to cover their tracks. That's all on that asshole."

"Still, I feel responsible."

"Mel," Vinnie said. "You are just a rung in the ladder of Jordan Brender's karma. I think of all the jerks we've handed over to the law, any of them could have done terrible things if we hadn't found them. You are not responsible for acts this man perpetrates."

"Mac," Rosa said.,"you've been kinda quiet here. Wanna weigh in?"

"I'm not sure we're right," I said.

"Que?"

"I want to go back out to Devin's place. Something's gnawing at me."

CHAPTER TWENTY-ONE

***

Yeah. It was an odd thing to do.

The police tape was still up around the site, and as expected, most of the area had been trampled. The shack was a blackened pile of rubble, some thrown into the driveway and jungle from a small explosion. The banana palm and part of the brush around the house was also scorched, but the fire hadn't gone far in the damp climate.

"Rosa? Would you mind waiting here at the car? I want to look around and…"

"You're going to look for tracks, aren't you?"

"I know it sounds crazy, but I have a hunch, which might just be crap, but I want to check it."

"I will trust your hunches any day, and your tracking has saved our lives on more than one occasion. Sic 'em, Mac!"

I pulled off my work shoes and put on the pair of moccasins I kept in my small duffle. I figured that moosehide-soled shoes would be pretty unique on Kauai, so I wouldn't have to worry about my own tracks as I looked.

Most of the tracks I found were the standard footwear. Tactical shoes that were unobtrusive, had Vibram lug soles that allowed officers to have the traction they needed when moving quickly was a necessity. Mixed in with these were almost-treadless dress shoe prints, which I was pretty sure belonged to the investigating detective. They had a slight rotation of the entire right foot whenever the owner had been walking with normal strides. I'd noticed that Detective Smith's body language indicated lower back pain. My guess was these were his prints.

Also, there were the prints of the larger insulated rubberized boots of the local firefighters. It took me about fifteen minutes to identify every track and assign them to whomever they might have belonged to.

I squatted and let my vision go wide and slightly blurry, trying to see everything in my field of vision while letting my mind relax. I had covered most of the driveway, and the area closer to the house. These were useless at this point, having been trampled as well as burned and flooded. I let my gaze drift toward the edges, the areas that someone might use if they were trying to sneak up on the home. Something caught my eye on the left side of the drive, which was below a slight hump in the hill, perfect for keeping a low profile behind.

Walking over, I saw faint tracks, a smooth finish front with a deep heel. The heel held a pattern I'd seen before. The boots were cowboy boots, Tony Lamas if I was not mistaken. And I wasn't.

Someone else had been here. The prints looked semi-fresh, with a few rain pocks but not much erosion. I followed them toward the house, and lost them in the sea of firefighter and police prints. The cowboy had been here first. There were a lot of cowboys on Kauai; it was a cattle ranching island.

But did these prints belong to one of them, or someone else? Someone dressing as a cowboy.

Someone with a pulled down Stetson, a denim outfit and a bushy bushy beard? Someone with a pair of military duffels? Couldn't be sure on a conscious level, but my gut was saying yes.

***

"I don't think Jordan Brender killed them," I said.

My pronouncement left Vinnie, Uncle Gil, Melinda, and even Duke all raising their eyebrows. Rosa, whom I'd confided my theory to on the way back to Duke's place was taking Graciella for a walk down to the river, something we'd both decided might be better while I spoke to the team.

"If not Brender, who the hell else could possibly be concerned with what we're doing here?" Uncle Gil asked.

"Who's our wild card? Who seems to show up at the most odd times and has a record that just disappears into thin air? Who most likely has those government skills and connections that have Graci, and quite honestly, myself, looking over our shoulders?"

"Martinelli?" Uncle Gil looked skeptical. "I'm not saying it's outside the realm of possibility, but why would he come here? Just to chase down Graciella? That'd be taking obsession to a whole new level."

"Who is this guy?" Duke stood, his face darkening.

"Graci's ex-boyfriend," I told him. "Also possibly a former government operator."

"At least we're assuming he's former," Vinnie said, "Government, that is."

"You're sure on the ex-boyfriend thing?"

"Part of the reason we brought her along in the first place," Vinnie assured him. "Dude's an a-hole. A scary one."

"Mac," Uncle Gil interrupted, "why Martinelli? I like the theory that Brender's old man called him, tried to shake the son down and found out his kid's a killer as well as a swindling scumbag."

"And then goes and eliminates the childhood friend because the old man told us about him," Vinnie said.

"That assumes a level of cold-bloodedness that is not yet in evidence with our man Jordan," I said. "But I want to assure you, looking into Martinelli's eyes as he attempted to choke the life out of me with his gorilla hands, that he is more than cold blooded enough."

"Still, Mac," Uncle Gil said. "What leads you to believe

it's him? I mean, is he that obsessed with Graciella that he'd go to the time and expense to track us down here? And how would he have known?"

"When he attacked me, he stole my messenger bag..."

"You said there was nothing in there to identify you."

"There wasn't, but Melinda's case notes were in there. Those notes spoke of a great deal of money, both hers and the association of victims of Brender. That's a lot of cash, and I'm sure Martinelli would have no qualms about forcing Jordan to tell him how to get access to it," I said. "But how to find the money man?"

"Follow the people already hunting him," Uncle Gil said.

"That's what I think. As was said, it's a whole lotta cash, and swindlers don't usually trust their local bank."

"And they are unlikely to call the cops if they're stolen from," Vinnie said.

Uncle Gil's head was lowered in thought. He rubbed his bristly chin and said, "You really think Martinelli might be using us as bird dogs to Brender?"

"Can't say I know for sure, but we found leads to Brender, mostly through a lot of hard hunting and luck. Maybe what we accomplished was more effort than Martinelli's assumed resources could provide. So what does he do? He finds and follows us to see if we can dig up what he needs. Like you said, we're his bird dogs."

"I dunno," Vinnie said. "That seems like a pretty complicated scenario. That Jordan knows we're after him and is trying to erase the trail seems more likely to me."

"If *we* find Brender, maybe Martinelli can get to him somehow and find out where all that money is. If not, Graciella is the consolation prize."

"But how the hell," Vinnie asked, "would he have found us?"

"When Rosa went to the Tri-Cities to get Graci, Martinelli

tried to chase them down, but they got away in Rosa's RAV. If, as we suspect, he was with the government, he surely would have gotten her license plate and once he has that, he had her name. Once he had her name, he could look through her records and find both her place of residence and her employer. My face will testify to the fact that he found her apartment."

"Once he had my employer, he might be able to find who else worked for said employer and whose phones to hack."

"And once he hacked our phones, he could follow our texts and maybe listen in to our calls. Shit," Uncle Gil said. "Everyone outside, now. Leave your phones here."

***

Uncle Gil walked us down Duke's driveway and we sat on some large volcanic rocks that had once been used as a quite substantial wall.

"Here is what we are going to do," he said. "Tomorrow, everyone is getting a trac-phone from our local Wal-Mart and we're going to pay cash for them. Then, we're going old school. We communicate through those phones only. If we need to pass information in a more permanent manner, we write it down on note pads. Are we clear on this?"

"Crystal," Vinnie told him.

"Also, I want to find some sweeping gear and go over the cars and Duke's house for electronic surveillance devices."

"Wait, what? You think my house is bugged?"

"It's possible, dude," Vinnie said. "Let's be sure."

"What about Graciella?" Duke asked.

Uncle Gil paused for a moment. "Tomorrow, Vinnie and I will take the van, and Graci will stay close to us anytime we are off this property. Melinda, will you ride with Rosa, Mac, and Mikey?"

"Anything I can do to be helpful," she said. "I sure wish I had my little .357 revolver, though."

"You and me both, sistuh," Vinnie said.

"I got a legal gun," Duke said, "Twenty-gauge shotgun. Gil, I'm ridin' with you tomorrow."

"What about work?" Vinnie asked.

"I own the business, and I got guys good enough to stand in for me working at the site. I can take a few days away," Duke said. "You think Mikey is in danger? Do I need to send him to his aunt on Oahu?"

"Your call. He might be safer there."

"Mike, we get back to the house, you pack your things. I'm gonna have Sonny take you over to your aunty Betty's." He paused. "Maybe we should send Graciella too."

"She won't go without Rosa, and Rosa won't go." I said. Duke looked down at his hands, a man more worried than he'd been in many a year.

"Mac, tomorrow, you, Rosa and Mel go and impart our Martinelli theory to your friend, Detective Smith. I'd also like for you to ask him if he knows any good P.I.s on the island."

"What do we need with a Private Investigator, Uncle Gil?" I asked. "We've all got licenses for that."

"Not in this state, you don't, but that's beside the point. I want someone to very discretely follow us. I want it done so discretely, that the PI will be able to see anyone else who might be following us. You get my meaning?"

"We'll essentially be bait to draw him out, assuming I'm right on this," I said.

"That's it. And if you're wrong, we continue with the search for Jordan Brender. We've still got nine days until our flight back to the mainland, and I feel like we're getting close. If we can just find Mama Brender, I'd bet we'll get our lead. Swindler guy and his mother seemed close, from what we were told, and I'd bet dollars to donuts that we can find a link from her to him."

CHAPTER TWENTY-TWO

***

I missed my smartphone already.

We had gotten up early to accomplish the tasks my uncle had set before us, and Rosa and I were just leaving the police HQ. We both carried disposable limited-minute phones from Wal-Mart and the only Internet access we had was through my iPad, which we had to find a hot spot for if we needed to research something.

Detective Smith had listened to my theory and my reasons for that theory. He was skeptical.

"So. This nut job supposedly follows you because he's got some sorta magical shadow government powers and is able to just hack into your phones. Gotta say, Mister Lugar, this sounds like a smokescreen to me."

"We're not saying we're positive, we're just saying it's a possibility. The guy had government intelligence connections and he knows all too much about the money involved with Jordan Brender," Vinnie told him.

"You've nothing to lose by keeping an eye out for him," I said. "He has several warrants out for his arrest now, and if we're right, he's here and willing to do whatever he has to, to find Brender and get that money."

Smith had two murders in two days on his hands, and he was willing to listen to anything that might bring the perpetrator to justice. He got photos from Martinelli's record in Richland and distributed them throughout the force with a warning about Martinelli's dangerous possibilities.

"If this Martinelli has followed you out here, he must have an assumed identity," Smith said. "With arrest warrants on his head, TSA should have scooped him up."

"If we're right about his connections, I doubt getting a false identity set up would be that hard for him," Rosa said.

"As if I don't have enough problems," Smith replied. "Just don't think I'm relaxing my watching of you bounty hunters though."

The KPD detective was even more skeptical about our request to find a PI, but had provided an address and phone number of a man he said knew his stuff. One who likely could help us sweep the cars and Duke's place for listening devices.

Rosa and I had been very quiet while we were in the car, speaking in single syllables most of the time and occasionally resorting to notes. We were doing our best to find the address we were seeking in Kapaa, and I was starting to think we should have brought a GPS, but I had no idea if Martinelli could hack one of those, too. We finally found the place, a tiny office on the end of a laundromat, coffee shop and mini-mart. Somehow, it seemed to fit the private investigator business perfectly.

"This is the place," I said as we stepped away from the rental sedan. "Tanaka said he'd meet us here."

"Doesn't look like the P.I. biz pays all that well," Rosa said, looking at the office with a disdainful eye.

"Small dingy offices are a requirement, Rosa. It's part of the mystique. Didn't you ever watch any of those old Bogart movies?"

"I figured since we're in the state of Hawaii, he'd be living in some rich guy's mansion."

"Hmmm. Good point."

We opened the door and were surprised to see a very well-ordered, almost sparse-looking space. A buddha sat on a small bureau in one corner, with flowers and tatami mat in front of it. On the mat was a meditation cushion. Somehow, I didn't think Tanaka would be wearing the prerequisite Fedora and trench coat.

"Hello," a deep mellow voice came from the room to the left. Tanaka emerged from the small bathroom for the office, drying his hands on a paper towel. He wore the regulation flowered button-up shirt that many businesses on the island thought of as a company uniform. He was not a large man, though he looked quite solid. His face was composed and showed no particular emotion.

"Mr. Tanaka, I presume," Rosa said.

"I am he. And you are Mr. Crow and Ms. Fernandez?"

"Yes, but please call me Rosa. This is Mac."

"Since we're going on a first name basis, please call me Terry. Have a seat and lets get down to brass tacks," Tanaka said. "From what Rosa told me on the phone, you are… bounty hunters?"

"That's correct. Part of a four-person team," Rosa told him. "We are searching for a gentleman who grew up on the island about twenty years ago, named Jordan Brender. A swindler who's conned close to two and a half million dollars from a group of seniors, taking their retirement savings."

"What a sweetheart. And you want me to help find him?"

"While we can use all the help we can get, what we really need is someone to watch our backs while we're on the hunt. This will probably require two operatives. And we also need a bug sweep."

"You have a four-person team, and you need me to watch your back? And someone has put listening devices on you?"

"We think so," I said. I told him about our two conflicting theories on who was listening in on us and Tanaka whistled when I finished.

"So we've either got a swindler who's perfectly content to kill not only his estranged father but also his childhood best friend; or you're being kept under surveillance by a psycho, possible ex-CIA guy who also has little regard for human life.

Does that about sum it up?"

"In a nutshell," Rosa said. "What we need is for you, and another operative you trust, to follow us, giving us plenty of room to find out if we are being followed by someone else. Photos of that someone else would be great, but we don't expect you to confront this person in any way. Just keep in touch with us, and let us know when we're being followed. We'll either confront the person or we'll contact the police."

"I know a few people who can help me out with tailing your group It's best not to have the same person following you around all the time. After a while it gets easy to spot the familiar face. When would you like to do the bug sweep?"

"We'd like to get our car done, the one outside. We also have a large van, and we'd like to have this address swept," I handed Tanaka a Post-it note with Duke's place of residence on it. "The door will be locked, but here is a key. No one should be there, but I will make sure everyone involved knows who you are."

"Anything else?"

Rosa looked at me and nodded.

"We could use a little help locating our guy's mother, Dianne Brender," I said, feeling a slightly embarrassed flush come to my face. "Normally, we can trace and track people pretty good, but we've lost her. We think she's on the island, remarried but we have no idea to whom, and for some reason, the records that would normally lead us where we need to go don't seem to be available. Someone who knows the local people and situations better than us mainlanders would be a big help. Her maiden name was Startzel."

Tanaka smiled, and I could almost hear the cash register sounds ringing in his head.

"Do you have time in your schedule to do all this, Terry?" Rosa asked.

"If you've got the money. I've got the time."

***

We'd left Melinda at the coffee shop, with a small digital camera that we'd picked up at Wal-Mart. It was a long shot, but there was always the possibility that our ghost would wind up compromising himself if he didn't know one of us was watching the car from behind the tinted windows of the Coffee Palace.

"Anything?" I asked her.

"I'm not a trained agent, but I didn't see anyone showing particular interest in us or the car," she replied.

"Maybe we should ask Tanaka to see if any other P.I.s he knows have been hired to follow us," Rosa said.

"I dunno," I said. "You'd think that a hired hand would just make things more complicated for 'em. Two people dead, any investigator worth their salt would realize that they might be working for a murderer."

"Maybe we should ask Tanaka if any of his fellow P.I.s have gone missing," I said. Both Melinda and Rosa looked at me with expressions of dismay.

"Yeesh, there's an awful thought," Melinda said. We watched as Tanaka took his equipment and entered our car, moving from one door to another. He'd barely been working five minutes before I saw him wave toward the coffee shop.

"He's found something," Rosa said.

"That was quick," I said. "Let's go see what we've got."

Because hope springs eternal, we left Mel in the shop, watching for anything suspicious. We walked over to Tanaka, who picked up his gear and motioned us into his office.

"You got good instincts, folks," he said. "Found not one, but two bugs. One under the dash, and one under a rear seatbelt attachment. I intend to go over the car again, but I wanted you to know your suspicions on this were dead on."

"Jeeze Louise! No wonder we kept getting there too late. We do half our planning and thinking in the cars," Rosa said.

"No wonder he always knew who to kill. But if he's using us as bird dogs, it doesn't help his cause to murder the people we need to interview."

"If it's Brender, that's just what he wants. If it's Martinelli, he probably thinks if he can get to the informant first, then he won't need us. Whether he gets the information or not, he has to eliminate all loose ends," I said.

"I think I will be extra careful on this job," Tanka told us. "So, you want me to strip out the bugs?"

"Maybe, but we do have an opportunity here," Rosa said.

"Misinformation?" I asked.

"Maybe a way to set a trap?" Rosa pondered.

"Make either Brender or Martinelli come to us."

"Might make our lives easier, one way or another."

"I'll call Uncle Gil, I think he might like that idea."

***

He didn't find any more bugs in the sedan, but all in all, Tanaka found three more bugs in the van, and none in Duke's house. The house being clean was surprising to me, and I decided to circle Duke's two and a half acres to see what I could find. I found two spots nestled back in the brush where someone had lain, and in the mud leading to them, cowboy boot prints. Tony Lamas.

Whoever he was, he knew where we lived.

"Ah, Jesus!" Duke yelled when I shared my findings. "He's fucking spying on us? Here? Damn glad I sent Mikey off island. I wish I'd sent Graci and Melinda with him."

We hadn't let Graciella know about my theory that her ex-boyfriend Martinelli might be the one following us. In retrospect, it was a mistake. Now that she knew, she was more than a little pissed about it.

"I go where I think I should go, okay? I'm perfectly safe here, Duke," she said. "And you don't send me anywhere. I'm sticking to Gil and Vinnie like glue during the day, and I got you prowling this house at night, like a security insomniac. Melinda and me, we're watchin' each other's backs."

"I'd feel a lot better doing that," Melinda said. "if I had my revolver rather than this pepper spray and these stun guns that Rosa gave us. I'm an American. I should be able to own a firearm here, like the second amendment says."

"We're in Rome," Uncle Gil told her, "We do like the Romans do. So, our shadow didn't bug the place, but has been sitting out in the brush, maybe with a listening dish. We need to nip this crap in the bud."

"What can we say to draw him out?" Vinnie asked. We'd decided to leave the bugs in the cars, being very careful of what we said and writing out anything we didn't want our tail to find out.

I had a very good thought, if my Martinelli theory was correct, what… or who, would be excellent bait to bring him out in the open, but I wasn't going to go there. Rosa and Duke both would have murdered me for even mentioning the idea.

"I guess the best thing would be to make him think we had a hot lead to Brender, and have someone else ready to pounce, or at least get photos of the jerk," I said. "We mention some childhood contact of Brender's, someone like that Glass guy, only without mentioning any names, and really play up that we've got the final piece to the puzzle. Maybe with Tanaka and his team's help we can spring the trap."

"We *will* want to apprise local law enforcement, specifically Detective Smith, as to our intentions," Rosa said. "Might make us a lot more popular with him."

"And might improve our chances, or make them worse. It depends on if Smith's crew can be discrete," Uncle Gil said. "While I welcome legal muscle backing us up, I don't want our prey to bolt because someone was obviously a cop."

CHAPTER TWENTY-THREE

***

Much to my surprise, Detective Smith was on board with the trap idea.

After meeting again with the police, Detective Nakamura volunteered to be bait. He was nondescript, and once out of his "plain clothes" suit and tie and into regular civilian garb, he actually looked like just another dude you'd see in a local park.

We pulled our original smartphones out of our suitcases, and began what I hoped was a convincing series of short calls and texts to each other. We were pretty sure either Martinelli or Brender had hacked our phones, and now we were putting that theory to the test. We'd also left the bugs in place, so one way or another, the info we wanted to drop would get to our murderer.

"Uncle Gil, have found a possible lead to finding Brender's mother."

"Details?"

"Local who says he went to school with B, and has done some landscaping for mama."

"Excellent work. When can we meet? Assume he wants payoff."

"Promised $400. Hope that's okay."

"We'll get it back from Brender. When's the meeting?"

"Two hours from now. Lydgate State Park in Kapaa. Meeting in the back picnic area. He'll be wearing a red shirt, blue shorts, red bandana as do-rag."

"Colorful."

"Will you be there? Supposed to meet at 2:30"

"Meet you there 2:15."

After that, we kept texting small inconsequential things, but not very often. I was worried we might have tipped off our ghost by having not used the phones for a day, but it was a chance we were willing to take. Rosa, Melinda and I pulled into the main parking lot at 2:00 p.m., and sat in our sedan, windows rolled down, watching people.

Families walked by, often with a gaggle of kids having a great time. For the most part, phones had been left in bags or cars and people were actually enjoying their time on Earth without electronic distraction. The ocean and the beach were irresistible.

A native-looking woman sat on a bench fifty yards down from us, dressed in shorts, flowery top and a sun hat. Unlike most of the other people there who were wearing flip-flops, she had on a good pair of running shoes and was sitting out in the sun reading the local paper. A small shoulder bag sat next to her, one just about the right size to hold a large frame handgun.

Cop.

I guessed that if I spent long enough, I could pick out others in the area who were just a little bit out of synch with everyone else. Most of Detective Smith's people were uniformed officers, being called into covert plainclothes action. I had no idea how much training they'd had at remaining unobtrusive.

I glanced at my phone. Two twenty. Uncle Gil was set in the parking lot fifty feet away. He and Vinnie were watching for anyone suspicious coming from the west. Nakamura was supposed to walk in to the meeting point from the east and sit as if waiting for us.

He was late.

Two thirty came, then two forty, and still no Nakamura.

I saw the cop lady glance at her watch, and a concerned look passed over her face. I had a bad feeling. I stepped out of the van.

"Mac!" Rosa said, "what are you doing?"

"Something's wrong. I feel it in my gut." Before she could say anything else, I started on foot toward the east parking lot, where Nakamura was supposed to enter. As I passed the undercover woman, I said from the side of my mouth, "Something's not right. Tell Smith there's a problem."

"Wait, dammit!" she said, yelling as quietly as humanly possible. I kept walking. Behind me, I heard gravel crunching, and saw Rosa trailing me, but not attempting to catch up. She literally had my back.

Reaching the far parking lot, I looked for our patriotically clad agent, and was halfway to the far end of the lot when I heard Rosa yell, "Mac! Look out!"

A beat-up looking pickup truck roared up from behind me, and I barely avoided being run over. The driver's side mirror slapped my shoulder as I dodged, spinning me around but the driver and I locked eyes as it happened. Huge beard, cowboy hat. It was the buff cowboy I'd seen in the baggage claim, and looking into his coal-black marble eyes, I flashed back to ridiculously strong hands choking the life out of me at Rosa's apartment back home.

"Stop!" I sprinted after the truck, and almost was able to get hold of the tailgate, but he gunned it as he left the lot, and left me in his dust.

"Mac!" I heard Rosa yell behind me. I saw her kneeling beside something lying behind a car and as I ran up, I saw it was Nakamura, his badge lying on the ground next to him. He was bleeding from a head wound, and Rosa was dialing 911 and asking the dispatcher for an ambulance. I got on my Wal-Mart phone and called Smith.

"Nakamura's down!" I probably needn't have bothered.

The police woman, having had both Rosa and me walk past her, had followed us both and was on a small hand-held radio. Less than thirty seconds later, we had five cops, including Smith, surrounding the downed officer.

"What the hell happened?" he said. The detective was pissed and worried for the partner he was kneeling over. He held a bandana to Nakamura's wound.

"It was Martinelli," I said.

"You're sure?"

"Yes. He was driving an old eighties era pickup that looked like it was half rust. License plate was BSGN 721. He turned toward Kapaa."

"Moki! Tom! Get your butts after him! Dwayne! Get every car in the area looking for that pickup!" The plainclothed cops scrambled for their cars. Within a minute, cars zoomed out of the lot, magnetic flashing blue lights on top.

"Ohhhh…. Geeze…" Nakamura groaned.

"Dave! Don't try to move. Ambulance is on the way."

"Son of a bitch came up on me the second I left my car. Had a freakin' machete!" Nakamura winced and lay his head back down. "Told me to get in his truck… or I'd be sorry."

"You can tell us at the ER, man."

"Pulled my gun and my badge, and damn all if he didn't slap my nine-mil out of my hand like some sort of gorilla! Hit me in the head with the butt of that… short sword and that's all I remember."

"You're lucky he didn't Musashi your head clean off."

"Where's my gun? Did he take my gun? Oh shit!"

"Here it is." I pointed under a Prius that was parked a few feet away. The weapon was far enough under the car that I'd had to crouch low to see it which was probably the only reason Martinelli hadn't taken it. I let the policewoman retrieve it, not wanting to get any new fingerprints on it.

"Oh, thank God," Nakamura said. No cop wanted their weapon to be used by a criminal. I was glad as well. If Martinelli was using a machete, it said he hadn't been able to smuggle a firearm onto Kauai. And for now at least, it looked like he was going to be resorting to more mundane forms of destruction.

"Crow," Detective Smith said. "I want your team at my office in one hour. Now that we know who, I want to see if we've got everything we can from you on this guy, and maybe to strategize a way to find him."

"We'll be there," I said. Then I noticed Uncle Gil standing just outside the circle of bystanders that was starting to gather. I looked at him, raising my eyebrows in question. He nodded. Rosa and I walked over and told him what had happened, though he'd figured out most of it from listening.

"Well," he rumbled in his gravelly voice. "At least we know who our killer is now."

***

An hour later, Uncle Gil, Rosa and myself were sitting in Smith's office. Vinnie, Duke and Melinda had taken Graciella to lunch to let her know the situation, and also to make sure that she was not alone. We weren't going to let her go unprotected until we had the son of a bitch.

And somehow, we were going to get him.

"So who the hell is this guy? Rambo?" Detective Smith asked. "We found the truck, which by the way was stolen from the airport, sunk halfway into the river with no trace of this Martinelli."

"Like we told you, the guy was very likely a government operator. Obviously, he's also very physically dangerous, and good at disguises."

"And somehow connected. All the bugs we found were not cheap crap. Very state of the art, and obviously, he had our phones hacked somehow." Rosa said. "This is not going to be some carjacker case, Detective. This guy is a professional, and he is one with no scruples to speak of."

"If you have no scruples, there are ways to get firearms on

this island, same as anywhere else. It ain't as easy as on the mainland, but if he gets a scrubbed gun, you might want to think twice before you try to chase down the vehicle he's in." Smith looked pointedly at me as he said it. "You might want to hesitate also, before you throw yourself in front of a group of police officers trying to catch a criminal. Cops first, bounty hunters second."

"Sorry, won't happen again." I could have brought up how we found their guy, identified Martinelli and called the ambulance before any of their team showed up, but Uncle Gil had slowly been making me realize the wisdom of choosing my battles.

"Don't make promises you can't keep, son," Smith said, looking down at his phone. "Text from Nakamura. Minor concussion but doctors say he'll be okay, thank God."

"Glad your guy is okay," Uncle Gil said. "That could have gone a lot worse, considering it's a pretty safe bet that Martinelli is the guy who whacked both Brender senior and Kalua. Any strategy for taking him down?"

"I'd love to set a trap for him, but I'm pretty sure he's gonna be hyper-vigilant from this point on," Smith said. "Best we can do is have my officers watch for any sign of him, try to find out where he's staying."

"He was on our flight," I said. Both Rosa and Uncle Gil looked at me with surprise on their faces.

"What?" Smith said. "You knew he was on the flight?"

"No. I just made the connection," That wasn't completely true, but now I had confirmation of my suspicions. I turned toward Rosa. "Remember the denim cowboy? He sat three seats back from us."

"I… uh," she said. "Wait! At the baggage claim! Short, huge beard, had a big grey Stetson kinda, covering his face… standing next to those two arguers!"

"That was him. I'm sure of it. No wonder I kept finding

cowboy boot prints. I'd guess that Martinelli has a favorite pair of Tony Lamas."

"I remember him now," Uncle Gil said. "Every time I'd head back to talk to you two, he'd be asleep with that hat over his eyes."

"So, he came in on your flight? Which was?" Smith asked.

"Alaska Air 122," Rosa told him. She fished in her small waist purse and brought out her boarding pass. She handed it to the detective.

"At this point, I'll take any lead I can get," Smith said. "I'll get my artist to Photoshop a dark bushy beard and a cowboy hat on the guy's mugshot and take it to the car rental place. We'll see if we can get anything usable from them or from the airline. It's not much, but it's something."

***

Getting into the car, which we'd removed the bugs from, Uncle Gil sat and looked thoughtfully at the horizon for a moment.

"I hate being played," he said.

"Obviously the guy has undercover skills," Rosa said.

"Yeah, that's what worries me. We need to up our game when it comes to situational awareness. We can't just…"

My uncle's burner phone rang. We'd shut down our smartphones and left them at Duke's once again. The only ones who knew the Wal-Mart phone numbers were either members of the team or…

"Tanaka! Any news for us?" Uncle Gil fumbled for a moment, looking for a speaker setting on the disposable cell phone, but finally we all just leaned in close and he turned up the volume.

"Mr. Chambers. I spoke with Vinnie Lugar about what went down at the park. Seems like your tail is the ex-CIA psycho, rather than the Swindler Psycho," Tanaka said.

"Yeah, 'fraid so. When you're following us, you might want to watch your own ass. Mister Martinelli is good with disguises, and wary as a fox."

"Great. Good to hear," Tanaka replied, "Actually, though I was calling about another matter you hired me for."

"You found more bugs?" Uncle Gil asked.

"Ah, no, the other matter."

My uncle looked at Rosa and I quizzically. "What other matter?"

"Your nephew had me looking for Brender's mother."

"Did he? He didn't tell me that. What's the word, then?"

"I have a current address for Mrs. Dianne Bourbonaise."

"And she is…"

"Yep. Formerly Mrs. Dianne Brender."

CHAPTER TWENTY-FOUR

***

Sometimes it's best to do these things early in the day.

Uncle Gil, Rosa, Melinda, and myself were outside the Bourbonaise residence at nine the next morning, dressed in our vests and dark tactical clothing. We weren't trying to overtly say we were with the police, but people dressed in the same general manner tended to get people's attention.

It also sometimes intimidated them into saying a bit more than they might have if we'd been dressed as Jehovah's Witnesses.

We sat and watched for a while, first. Partly because it's always good to get the lay of the land in any enterprise like this, and partly because we were being a bit hyper-vigilant ourselves, not knowing if Martinelli might have some way of keeping tabs on us we didn't know about.

"Nice place, not too ostentatious," I said. "Kinda modest for the location." We were on the west end of Hanalei, sitting outside a row of houses next to a gorgeous beach.

"Duke took me out in his cousin's boat last night," my uncle said. "These homes back right up to the ocean and if you ran out the back door, across the lawn and a short shelf of rock you'd be swimming in the Pacific. Guess how much this little place goes for, in all likelihood."

"No idea."

"Roughly a million, seven."

"Holey Hannah!"

"I keep telling you; location, location, location. You want

to live on the ocean, you gotta be rich. Most of the natives here don't live on the ocean on their own island."

"I'm guessing if you're native," Rosa said, "and your family hasn't owned beachfront for generations, you're probably not going to unless…"

"Unless you're rich. Natives at least get some tax breaks, but kids comin' up have a hard time making enough to live."

"Sounds like no one's gonna have beachfront unless they're rich."

"Pretty much. All right, we've sat here long enough. Let's do this," Uncle Gil said. He entered a number into his Trac-phone. "Tanaka? We're going in. Keep a discrete eye out for our boy. Good. Thanks."

We got out of the van and walked up to the house. We had brought Melinda, in case the mother decided that her little angel couldn't have done all those mean things we were accusing him of. Mel planned on setting her straight with gusto.

"Rosa, you comin'?"

"Be right with you. Wanna check something." She moved up the street.

Uncle Gil, Melinda, and I walked onto the porch, which had some wicker furniture I recognized from our last trip to Costco, and rang the bell.

After a short wait, a voice came from inside the door. "Who is it?"

"Ms. Bourbonnais, my name is Gil Chambers. We need to speak with you on a legal matter of some importance. Can you come out and talk to us?"

"What sort of matter?"

"It concerns your son, Jordan." He showed her his ID through the peephole. Our I.D.s are legit. They also have a vague resemblance to federal I.D.s. Not our fault if people make assumptions.

The door opened, and an attractive middle-aged woman

stepped out, suspicion on her face, which I guess was reasonable. We certainly didn't have her baby boy's best interests at heart. She obviously had spent a lot of time and money to look immaculate, her blond hair perfectly cut to accentuate cornflower blue eyes. She looked at Gil and me in our tacticals, then at Melinda in her flowered print top and shorts. We were, admittedly an odd-looking combination.

"What is this about?" she asked.

"We are looking for Jordan, ma'am," Uncle Gil told her. "He has several arrest warrants out for him across a variety of states. I'm afraid your son is alleged to have bilked a fair number of elderly victims out of their retirement savings in a fake investment scam. He's hurt a lot of people. We want him to come in with us and answer these charges."

"You said allegedly."

"Innocent until proven guilty in a court of law. However, Jordan has not exactly been faithful to that system, avoiding numerous summons and warrants by fleeing when people find out what he's doing."

"No," she said, shaking her head. "My son would never do anything like that."

I casually walked over and stood in front of the door she had closed behind here. Glancing down to my right, I could see Melinda's blood was starting to boil. I hoped we could prevent mayhem, but I wasn't going to try and hold her back too much.

"If your son is innocent of these charges, he needs to come in, address them and clear his name," Uncle Gil told her. "Do you know where he is? We believe he's on Kauai."

"Well, you're wrong there," she said, looking down and away. Her response was quick; she wasn't a great liar. "And he doesn't ever contact me anyway. I haven't heard from him in years."

"Then how do you know he hasn't returned? We have more than a little evidence that he has," I said.

People don't like being tripped up, and she glared at me.

"Mrs. Chambers, it doesn't really help anyone for him to avoid his… responsibilities. If he doesn't address this, he will be on the run for the rest of his life," Uncle Gil said. "If he comes in, faces the music, makes restitution and gets a good lawyer he could eventually be free of this, perhaps with limited time incarcerated."

"Who are you kidding? Are you even police officers?"

"We are licensed fugitive retrieval agents…"

"I know what that means! You're fucking bounty hunters, trying to make money off my son's misery!"

"Your son's misery!?" Melinda shouted. The genie was out of the bottle now. "Your son took ALL of my retirement! If I hadn't had friends willing to let me stay with them, I'd have to live in my car! He did this to HUNDREDS of people who had saved up most of their lives and just wanted to stretch their old age money a little. Your son's misery? Your son is a goddamn monster!"

Her vehemence made the woman take a step back from Melinda, who was shaking with fury. I had no intention of reining her in either, remembering the look on my own mother's face when she had to tell us her retirement had been stolen.

Mrs. Bourbonaise tried to head back into the house, but I just happened to be in her way.

"All these people's lives ruined, because she couldn't raise a decent son," Melinda said. "And now, she doesn't give a shit who the bastard has hurt, as long as little Jordan gets away without any punishment. Probably been that way all his life!"

"You people get off my property! Get out of here, or I will call the police!"

"That could be interesting," I said, stepping between the two women. "As a matter of fact, a Detective Smith of the KPD is very interested in talking to you regarding Jordan, also. So… go ahead. Make the call."

She glared at me once again and said, "I don't know where

my son is. End. Of. Story." She stepped around me and slipped into the slightly open doorway. I heard the deadbolt click to the locked position.

"I'm going to tell them all!" Melinda yelled through the door. "I'll give the entire group of people that your son screwed over your address and phone number! See how long until you grow a conscience!"

"Well," Uncle Gil said, "that could have gone better." He turned toward the van.

"I take it La madré didn't have much to say," Rosa said. She moved from where she'd been leaning against the van, watching the neighborhood.

"Yeah. We're boned," I said. "She's gonna protect her baby boy, no matter how much of a crap bag he is."

"Is this the end of the line, then?" Melinda asked, stricken. "Is this my fault?"

"No, Mel…" I started.

"Not the end of the line," Rosa said, pointing up the street to a mailbox on the end of Mrs. Bourbonnaise's property. The light of my life pulled an envelope out of her tactical vest and handed it to Uncle Gil.

"Well," Uncle Gil said, the beginnings of smile starting on his face. "Well, well, well."

"What is it?" Melinda asked.

"Maybe the final piece of the puzzle, if we are very lucky."

***

I am well aware that it is a crime to tamper with the mail, and so is everyone else on our team. But if we're going to have full disclosure here, bounty hunters have a bit more leeway than the average Joe.

We are also sneakier.

The envelope that Rosa had handed Uncle Gil was return addressed from Poipu, no name for the sender. Uncle Gil flicked open his spring-assisted folding knife and with a finesse

I didn't realize he possessed, carefully separated the glued part of the envelope. The flap had been shut carelessly enough that only a few sections held it closed. He pulled out a short one page note, with a check for $8,000 dollars.

The note read:

Here's a little something for expenses, we need to get together for coffee next Thursday. -J

The check was from a James Binder.

Binder. Brender?

By the time the envelope had been re-sealed and returned to the mailbox, we were all smiling.

CHAPTER TWENTY-FIVE

***

Poipu is a beautiful area, which is why the tourists love to flock there. Palm trees, cacti, beaches and upscale shopping abound. We were pretty sure we had our man's address, but we had no way to be completely sure.

I had gone online the previous evening, and scoured every record I could find on James Binder, and in a short time, I had a complete address. Further searching showed that the residence had been purchased and paid for in full only six months before. There were no photos of Binder, no driver's license, no Facebook or Twitter accounts. I really hoped we'd been extremely lucky, but there was a chance this was not our guy. But who sends someone $8,000 expense money out of nowhere?

The next day, we drove past the Prince Kuhio Park, down the road to where a number of nice homes sat on the edge of the ocean. Some of them were vacation homes. These were places where people were either lucky enough to own them for years, or were rich enough to afford oceanfront property. They had their place in the sun. Many of these same homes were rented out for a good portion of the year to people who could only afford a place in the sun for a week or two.

"Okay, this is the place," Uncle Gil said.

Half a mile down from the Hawaiian Prince's memorial, a very nice house, not a mansion by any means, stood in the bright Hawaiian sun. It was a two-story, with a colonial-style porch around the base and tall windows all the way around.

Coconut palms shorn of nuts swayed gently in the ocean breeze and a native lava-rock wall almost six feet high stood between the house and the street. A wrought-iron gate opened onto the street, and a hefty padlock was on the gate to keep out riffraff like us.

"Keep your eyes peeled. We cleared the van and the car of bugs, but Martinelli is too clever by far," my uncle told us. "I wouldn't put it past that bastard to have backup plans to trace us."

"Or beat us to the punch," Vinnie said, a grim expression on his normally cheerful face.

The street was colorfully gorgeous, as much of Kauai is on the surface. Locals in pickups headed to the little park/marina another couple hundred yards down the road, landscapers scurried around maintaining the perfect manicured look for some of the nearby homes, a utility truck made sure that everyone had the best Internet and a steady stream of brightly clad tourists walked up and down the street to various rentals and hotels. Most looking at the oceanfront homes and thinking "If I won the lottery…"

We'd brought both vehicles, and the entire group was with our team. We'd also brought Melinda, Duke, and Graciella, assuming safety in numbers and they sat in the van while we donned our tac-gear. One of Tanaka's people, a large young native man I hadn't met, parked less than a quarter mile from us to watch our backs.

"Uncle Gil," I said as we approached the wrought-iron gate, "Is that padlock unlatched?"

"Sure looks like it," he rumbled in his gravelly voice. "That can't be standard operating procedure. Everyone, be on your guard."

We moved up to the gate, leaving our friends in the vehicle, and went in tight against the wall. All of us were feeling naked without our firearms, a stun-gun being a poor substitute.

"Gil," Rosa said quietly, gesturing with her chin. "Camera. Looks like it's broken."

She was right. The camera, one of the older boxy models, was pointing straight down toward the grass. As we moved through the gate, I saw that it had been struck a hard blow with something sharp. Small amounts of wiring peeked out from the corner of its casing. Vinnie raised his eyebrow, and signaled for us all to approach silently.

We moved quickly across the well-tended lawn, past a fountain with decidedly well-endowed cherubs, and came onto the porch. The front door was ajar. Usually not a good sign.

"Hello!" Uncle Gil called out. "Mr. Binder! Are you in there?"

"I thought I heard something," I said. "A groan?"

"We're going in," Uncle Gil told us. "Gloves on, don't touch anything you don't have to. Got a bad feeling about this."

My uncle's instincts for danger and trouble were, as usual, right on.

"Gilbert! On the floor, next room," Rosa whispered.

It was a body, the body of a young man, early twenties. He lay there, clad in a Red-Dirt T-shirt and a pair of lime-green Speedos that left little to the imagination. One flip-flop sandal hung askew from his left foot.

"Human necks don't bend that way, do they?" I said, already knowing the answer.

"Not in my experience," Vinnie replied. "Look at the bruising on the neck, there."

"Martinelli."

"A good bet," Rosa said, rising from where she'd checked for a pulse. She put her leather gloves back on. "Body's still warm. Can't have happened long ago."

"Let's find Brender, if he's still here." We fanned out through the building. Very tasteful paintings hung on the walls, many of them involving what looked like Venice or Paris.

Kauai was also represented, but I guess when you can see the beauty every day, you don't need to have it on your walls.

"First floor is clear," Uncle Gil's voice quietly came over my radio. As he said that, a groan and a sob came from up a nicely furnished spiral staircase. We moved up the stairs, passing a very ornate chandelier hanging over the stairwell, and onto the upper floor.

We heard a soft moan come from a partially opened door and found a man sprawled on the bloody ornate bathroom tile. Had it not been for the fine white-blonde hair, I don't think I would have recognized John Binder, a.k.a. Jordan Brender. He had been severely beaten, and his brows and eyelids were swollen like a pro boxer at the end of a bad fight.

I winced when I noticed two of the fingers on his left hand were bloody stumps, ending at the first knuckle, and blood pooled around his hand and filled the gaps in the tile. On his chest, part of a smiley face had been deeply incised with something sharp. I was amazed he was still conscious. The pain must have been immense.

"Jordan?" Rosa bent down to him and spoke to him in the kindest voice I think I've heard. "Are you awake? Who did this to you?"

"Oh… God!" he said, half sobbing the words. "Please, help me."

"We're calling an ambulance, right now," she said, gesturing for Uncle Gil to do that very thing. "Was it a man with dark hair, with eyes very dark?"

"Oh…. Yes. He… His eyes, like Death." I was now sure it was Martinelli. "He killed Erik. Like a pit-bull grabbing a chihuahua. Snapped his neck… oh, why did Erik open that damn door?"

"What did he want from you? Why did he torture you?" Vinnie asked. Brender looked up at him, seeming to realize for the first time that we were strangers.

"The money of course. Took all I had at the house,

tortured.... me to get my passwords and the com... combination to the big safe," he said, his voice growing weaker.

I pulled out the bandage I keep in my vest, and gently wrapped his fingers, staunching the steady drip of blood. For all that he'd done, I wouldn't have wished horror like this on anyone, even Brender.

"Jordan, how long ago did this happen?" Rosa asked.

"I'm not sure," he said. "Seems like he was just here, but... I've been drifting in and out when the pain gets so bad..."

"Vinnie," Uncle Gil said, "you and Mac check the house. Let's make sure that the son of a bitch isn't hiding in some room waiting to jack us. Stay together."

Vinnie and I moved from room to room, and we were both missing our Glock pistols terribly. We had expandable batons, stun guns and pepper spray, but having something that would stop Martinelli in his tracks would have made me a lot more comfortable.

We checked the bedrooms, each decorated in a different and expensive style. All were immaculate, with the exception of one, which held surfboards, guitars and a fairly good selection of gaudy bling. The most impressive video game system I'd ever seen decorated half of one wall with speakers and a huge TV.

"Erik's room," I said.

"Yeah," Vinnie replied. "I'd guess so."

My Wal-Mart phone rang in my pocket. The screen wouldn't tell me who was calling, but as soon as she spoke, I knew it was Melinda and she was in a panic.

"Mac! It was Martinelli! He clobbered Duke from behind and took Graciella! He was in the utility service van!"

"Shit. We'll be right out! Vinnie! Martinelli jacked Duke and took Graci!"

We ran back to the bathroom and told Uncle Gil and Rosa.

"Get after him! Rosa, go with them, I'll tend to Brender,"

he said. "Keep updating me, so I can update KPD. Move! He's getting away!"

We burst out into the bright daylight and Duke was sitting in the driver's seat, a gash in his forehead. Melinda was trying to tie up a bandana to staunch the blood.

"Mel! Go in and help Uncle Gil," I said.

"I wanted to stop him," she cried out. "But he had a machete. I couldn't…"

"No time! Go!" Duke yelled. "We'll get her back."

Mel headed for the front door, while Rosa, Vinnie, and I piled into the van. We'd barely gotten seated before Duke was tearing up the road in hot pursuit. We passed Tanaka's operative, his car smashed on one side and the man himself holding his head. It didn't surprise me a bit that Martinelli had used his own van as a weapon.

We dashed past the park for Prince Kuhio, and blasted through the roundabout, getting honked at but leaving all the other vehicles intact. Barely. We burned up the short road to old Koloa Town and as we approached the T in the road, I could see people helping other people up from the ground near the crosswalk.

"Which way did he turn?" I yelled out the passenger window. "It was a utility van, right? Which way, right or left?" A woman tentatively pointed to the left and we turned west toward Wiamea.

"How the hell did he find Brender before us?" Rosa asked as we sped up the road.

"No flippin' idea," Vinnie replied. "We got no idea what resources he's drawin' upon. I thought Tanaka found all the bugs, but I might be wrong or hell, maybe he's watching us with a friggin' spy satellite."

That seemed pretty farfetched to me, but Martinelli had stayed ahead of us the entire time, so I wasn't going to discount anything. As we came to the point where the side road met the

Koloa Highway, the main road through most of Kauai, we saw a delivery truck on its side, and white powder all over the road. A man sat by the road, on his cell, but I didn't need to ask him where the van went. There was only one set of tire tracks and they veered left again, still heading towards Wiamea. Glancing down at the powder, I saw a canine track that must have been made moments before.

It looked very familiar.

It was a harrowing ride. Duke, angry with himself for letting Graciella be taken, was not by any semblance obeying the rules of the road. As I updated Uncle Gil on our location and orbital path, we passed cars in spots that almost made me crap my pants. Many horns were honked, and at least one sedan wound up in the ditch to avoid us.

We finally came to a long straightaway, and Duke's insane driving paid off. At the far end of the straight stretch we saw the other van, just rounding a corner.

"There he is!" Duke yelled and floored it. A quick glance at the speedometer saw us over ninety-five MPH, about forty miles per hour over the speed limit posted. I couldn't help but think that if one of Kauai's numerous roosters walked out in front of us now, that tiny impact would be enough to send us flying into someone's cow pasture.

We kept at it, and slowly seemed to be gaining, seeing the other van occasionally far ahead of us. We passed the turnoff to Port Allen, where Brender's childhood friend had been murdered and I felt a slight tingle along the back of my neck.

Coming around a long curve, we once again came to a straightaway, this one much longer than the first. The road ahead was completely empty except for a tour bus which passed us going the other way.

Martinelli had disappeared.

***

"He must have turned off at Port Allen," I said. "I have a strong feeling that's what happened."

"Duke, turn us around and go back," Rosa said.

"What if Mac's wrong?" Duke said, not taking his eyes off the road.

"I trust Mac's gut feeling more than I trust my local news," she said. "Turn around!"

"God, help us, I hope you're right," Duke said, turning the van around in a wild maneuver that threw red dust up in a cloud. "Maybe he's got a boat?"

"I was wondering what he was gonna do once he got past Waimea," Vinnie said. "There's not much beyond there but the missile facility and Polihalé State Park. The roads to the observatories are gated with big metal gates. Nothing but the Na Pali cliffs after that. And barely any way to get up them from this end of the island."

"That's why the old people lived back there," Duke said.

We came to the turnoff to Port Allen, and drove the short lane down to the waterfront, passing gift shops and several tourist boat-ride businesses. At a dirt parking lot, Duke took a right and headed toward what looked to me like the main marina. As we got closer to the dock, I noted a boat heading out of the harbor and turning west.

"Look! That's him! How the hell did he get a boat already?"

"And where the hell's he gonna go?" Duke mused. "That little speedboat ain't gonna get him far, and the only island he could reach from here would be Ni'ihau, the Forbidden Island, and he sure as shit ain't gonna get a warm reception there," Vinnie said.

"Does it matter?" Rosa said with heat in her voice. "By the time we can get a boat of our own rented, he'll be long gone with Graciella and with his connections, probably never have to stand trial for kidnapping her or killing Brender's boyfriend, Eric."

"Oh ye, of substandard faith," Duke said. "You think ol' Duke's lived on this rock all these years and he don't have connections? My cousin Sonny got a boat right at this here Marina. Lets me use it to go fishing. Hopefully it's gassed though…"

Duke parked the rental on a stretch of grass that was obviously not intended for the purpose, and was headed for the dock, shotgun in hand, before the rest of us could even extricate ourselves from the van. We grabbed our vests, but I wondered what the heck good our little array of stun guns and pepper spray were going to do us if Martinelli had an illegal handgun. I said as much to Rosa as we hurried up the dock.

"Way I look at it," she said, "he killed that guy with his bare hands and clobbered Duke with the butt of that machete. Would have been much easier to simply shoot 'em. My guess is that for all his fancy connections, he still hasn't come up with a firearm, and it's almost impossible to smuggle one in on an airliner now."

"I've had his hands around my neck, and I think he just enjoys using them to hurt people. He's got a grip like a steel worker. But he still could have stolen a gun."

"Well," she said, anger in her voice. "what do you think we should do? You ready to give up and let him go with Graci dragged behind him?"

"Hell no," I said, shoplifting a five-foot wooden pole with a fish gaff on the end from a boat we passed. "But we need to be careful as hell. Duke's old double-barrel shotgun has a serious range deficit compared to even a nine-mil. handgun."

"Amen to that," Vinnie said, coming up behind us to the boat Duke was working on starting. Sonny, Duke's cousin, evidently wasn't that much into appearances. The small fishing boat, named the *Kekemapa Nai'a* was rusty at numerous points that looked important to this landlubber. Duke cursed from where he stood at the wheel.

"What is it, Duker?"

"We gotta gas up before we can get going. Sonny don't leave it with a lot in it, had this bucket stolen once, and the only reason they caught the gal was that she ran outta gas."

"Shit. How long's that gonna take, bro?" Vinnie asked.

"You got a card, man, take us ten minutes, tops. But we gotta hook up now."

"I got a card. Let's do it!"

We pulled up to the nautical equivalent of a gas station, and began to fill the tanks. Martinelli had cleared the point and was out of sight. I held ropes on the gas dock while Rosa apprised Gil, then the cops, of the situation. As soon as Duke said full, Vinnie was replacing the nozzle and we all hopped in. After a moment of coaxing, Sonny's boat roared toward the harbor mouth.

"Police boat is clear up by Kappa. He'll be halfway to Fiji before they get here," Rosa said.

"Guess it's all us then."

Five minutes later, we had cleared the point, turned west and Vinnie was using my uncle's powerful binoculars to scan the ocean ahead for Martinelli. I was actually surprised when Duke yelled for everyone to grab something and the boat surged ahead, engines roaring in a way I hadn't expected from the beat up fishing boat. Vinnie started to fall back but Rosa, who was sitting, managed to get a hand on his back and kept him from hitting the deck.

"Thanks, thought I had my sea legs. Guess I'm outta practice."

"*De nada,* Vinn," Rosa said, as Vinnie began scanning the horizon again. "You see him?"

"No, I don't see him, dammit!"

"Vinnie!" Duke yelled back, dodging the spray from a swell we were blasting over. "There ain't nowhere he can go in that runner that's far enough out. It just don't have enough fuel capacity. I'm gonna burn for the Na Pali and see if he's gone that way. Maybe he's meetin' someone in a bigger boat!"

"What does he mean by 'burn'?" Rosa said as the boat leapt ahead even faster than we'd been going before. Evidently judging the *Kekemapa Nai'a* by its appearance was a mistake. We slammed into swells and went up and over them. Duke wasn't trying to be gentle, and I felt my stomach begin to do funny things. Not funny-ha-ha type things. Rosa was starting to look a little green, too.

We ran along the shoreline of the western side of Kauai, passing an old factory of some sort, then a town near the mouth of a huge river canyon, which I assumed was Waimea Canyon. We moved along fast enough that spray came over the bow every few minutes, and everyone was soaked. The breeze from our passage blowing over wet clothing didn't help much.

"I thought Hawaii was supposed to be warm!" I yelled.

"Just one of those days, bro!" Duke yelled back, a grim, set look on his face.

We moved west with the shoreline, rising and falling as swells came at us from the port bow, seaward side. I did my level best to keep an eye on the horizon or on the passing beaches to our right. After a time, my stomach evened out and I started to look through the various nooks and crannies of the boat to see if there was some kind of weapon that might serve better than a fish gaff.

I found a flare gun, a set of fins, a single fin, masks and one snorkel. There was a fourteen-inch billy club for braining fish, and several beer cans. There was also some fishing gear, but I doubted we were going to be able to snag our quarry and reel him in. None of these were going to be a lot of help if Martinelli had somehow managed to obtain a firearm on the island.

"Mac," Rosa said, "I think I'm gonna hurl." She'd been a little green a few minutes before, but now she was really looking bad.

"Aim her off the stern, Mac!" Duke yelled over his shoulder. "Go for a new distance record, Rosa! Maybe the fishing'll be good here tomorrow!"

Rosa stood, just to one side of the engines above a little ramp that led into the water. She was valiantly trying to hold it together but it looked to be only a matter of time. She leaned against the rear gunwale, knees partially bent, while steadfastly looking at the horizon trying to delay the inevitable.

"Rosa, if you need to…"

"Don't… make me talk," she said. "I'm doing my best to…" and that was it. She pushed her head out over the ocean and did an admirable job of mostly missing the boat. Seeing the long flying stream made my own throat start to quiver and the next swell, I knew what was going to happen. I joined Rosa in chumming the Pacific, though when I puked, I got a bit more on the engines than she did.

"Nice barfing, kids!" Vinnie said. I tried to come up with a snappy comeback, but Rosa, always more to the point just looked up from where she leaned on the rail and flipped him off.

"I feel better now that I've done it," I said.

"Good for… you," Rosa said. She still looked a little green but not as bad as a few minutes earlier. I patted her shoulder, and moved up to Vinnie who was still scanning the forward horizon, looking for Martinelli.

"Anything?" I asked.

"Naw, but we still haven't come around to the Na Pali yet," he said. "Coming' up on Polihalé State Park, now."

I looked off to our right and saw the end of what looked like some sort of military installation, followed by what looked like the wildest beach I'd seen on the island. Coming toward us, the flat land that we'd been running along gave way to sharp rising cliffs and on the top I could see what looked like astronomical observatories.

I got a bottle of water out of the small cooler by the wheel, and holding it above my mouth took some in. A fast spit into the ocean and my mouth wasn't so horrible anymore. Rosa opened her mouth and I poured some in for her. Using my bandana, we both cleaned up a bit.

"Thanks," she said. "I don't think I've got anything else left to puke. It does feel a little better."

"Hey Rosa!" Duke yelled from the wheel. "Check it out, point blank, starboard side! This'll make you forget your stomach."

Suspicious, we looked over the side, and saw a shape keeping pace with the fishing boat. I wasn't quite sure what I was seeing until the sleek shape surfaced and a plume of spray shot from it.

"Dolphins," she said, with such wonder in her voice that I instantly fell in love with her all over again. The one in front of us was not alone. Several of them played around the bow of the boat, crossing in front and seeming to chase each other under and along side of us.

For a moment, we forgot about the dangerous psycho we were following, the dead man back at Brender's home and even Graciella. There was just us, and these amazing wonderful creatures, who for some strange reason wanted to spend a few minutes traveling with us. Many people see dolphins around Kauai, but this moment made us feel as if the Universe was smiling on us and I prayed it was a good omen for Graci.

"Maybe it's a good omen," Rosa said, making me wonder if she was psychic. "If we get Graci back that's all I care about, even if we don't take down Martinelli."

"That will be our primary goal, Rosa. We will get her back. That bastard is not taking her with him."

Rosa grew silent and we looked at the point where the land turned around to the north side of the island. As we rounded that point, the dolphins vectored away and headed toward the west shore. The wind changed, and was now coming in from the sea, and Duke was obviously working hard trying to keep us on a straight course.

"I still don't see him. Maybe he went out toward the ocean and is meeting a bigger boat out there," Vinnie yelled to Duke.

"Nope," Duke replied. "Hey Mac! Mr. Tracker Man! Whatchoo see right there off the starboard bow?"

"It almost looks like a… smooth trail in the water. What is that?"

"Hydrostatic pressure caused by a boat going through the water. Takes a little time for the wake to equalize with the rest of the ocean, and I only see one other boat out here, and that ain't its wake."

Looking out to sea, I saw a single catamaran, loaded with tourists and heading back the way he had just come. Evidently the rough sea had made the commercial captains decide the trip just wasn't worth all the seasick passengers.

"You think that trail is him?" Vinnie asked.

"If'n it ain't, then we lost the son of a bitch, bro!"

CHAPTER TWENTY-SIX

***

I stood near the bow, watching the jagged trail of flattened water that led toward the Na Pali cliffs with every fiber of my being. We all knew this was a last resort. If it was Martinelli's wake, we might be able to stay with it before it dissipated in the rolling waves. If it was just another fisherman, then our only chance was if we somehow, by luck, overtook our quarry and saw him from a distance. At the moment, all we could do was sit and hope.

"Ain't that some view?" Vinnie asked.

"It looks very familiar."

"Pretty much any movie with big monsters on an island or pirates has used shots of the Na Pali Cliffs to show how remote the setting is."

"No wonder I recognize it," I said, following our trail with hawk eyes. "Duke! The trail is kinda turning toward the shore on that beach with the rock arch."

"Oh shit. Oh no, he di'n't," Duke said, staring intently towards where I was pointing. "Fucker!"

"What is it?" Rosa asked.

"That's a sacred beach. Kings used to be buried there, and no one is allowed to go there without a permit!" Duke angled the boat toward the beach, putting us at only a little above idling. The waves instantly began pushing us inward toward the beach.

"There!" Rosa yelled. "Just behind the arch on the first section of beach."

Looking there, I saw the runabout that Martinelli had either rented or stolen from Port Allen. Even at this distance, I could see two sets of tracks leading up from the waterline. As I watched, a large breaker rolled in and hit the runabout, driving it farther up on the beach and nearly rolling it over.

"That obviously ain't his boat!" Duke said.

"Can we land on that beach?" I asked.

"Only if you want Sonny to lose his fishing boat and his livelihood," Duke said. "Or, to put it another way, no, we'd probably wreck in this surf and maybe lose all hands. But I could try it… for her."

We all watched the big waves roll into the shore. The small boat took another hit and went up on its side. I thought I saw debris in the water.

"Is there a life raft or something we can go in on?" Rosa said.

"Ah, no. Sonny loses the boat, he figures he could swim to shore. He don't venture out too far, an' he's a pretty strong swimmer. Rafts cost money."

"Duke," I said over the wind blowing shoreward. "How close can you get?"

"I don't want to get any closer than a hundred yards, man. Those waves ain't kiddin' around!"

"Get us as close as you can."

I kicked off my shoes and began to rummage through the slop chest I'd looked through earlier.

"Mac, what are you doing?" Rosa said, her voice rising.

"You know what I'm doing, baby," I said, pulling on and tightening one of the fin sets I'd seen earlier. I slipped out of my vest and pulled on a mask and snorkel.

"No. No, Mac. You are not going into that surf!"

"He's about half crazy, Rosa, but if we want to keep Martinelli from taking Graci," Vinnie said, pulling on the other mask, "we got to risk big."

"No! Vinnie! Shit! That looks like suicide!"

Vinnie looked toward shore. "Naw, me and Mac're both strong swimmers, 'specially with the fins and masks. We'll practically be able to body surf in." He gave her the hang loose hand sign.

"This is as close as I go!" Duke yelled.

"Mac, this is crazy. Don't do it!"

"Someone's got to, Rosa. You're the hard charger on land, but I'm the better swimmer by far."

"No, you'll drown, Mac! And if you make it, I won't be able to back you up."

"What does Vinnie think?" I asked. Rosa turned toward Vinnie to get him to shut down this crazy idea. She was going to be pissed at me, but I grabbed the gaff, and slipped over the side.

***

Rosa had been worried for a reason.

I hit the water and instantly felt currents trying to take hold of me. I aimed myself toward shore and began kicking the fins furiously, trying to torpedo in as fast as possible. I felt like a bit of a shit-head, because I'd taken both fins and the snorkel. Vinnie had grown up in this ocean, while I'd spent most of my swimming time in lakes and rivers. I hoped, if he followed me, that his superior experience would carry him through with one fin and no snorkel.

What hadn't looked that far in the boat, seemed like miles through the tiny above-water area the mask allowed me to see. I timed my breaths through the snorkel to coincide with the back side of the waves as they passed me. It then struck me, as a large fish swam past, that I didn't really know the shark situation here on the island. I hoped I didn't look too much like an epileptic seal as I struggled toward the shore.

A particularly contrary wave broke over me well before it should have and I was crushed down into the deep blue depths.

I couldn't tell up from down for a few moments. I hadn't had a chance to pull in a fresh breath of oxygen and I had to mentally work hard to not panic. I soon oriented myself and kicked hard to the surface.

Air never tasted as sweet, even through a rubber tube.

Looking back, I couldn't see the boat, and I couldn't see Vinnie behind me anywhere and I hoped he was okay. It looked like I was on my own.

I dodged urchin-covered rocks, trying my best not to leave a trail of blood in the water. Eventually, there was nothing but sand beneath me, and I semi-body surfed to the beach on a large wave that deposited me on the sand with little regard for my well-being. As I sat there half-stunned, another wave hit me, knocking me ass-over-teakettle and tried to pull me back into the raging surf.

I quickly shucked my fins and threw them up on the beach. Coughing seawater, I half-ran and half-crawled out of the surf, leaving my gear above the high-water mark. The only thing I carried now was my folding knife and the fish gaff staff. I looked back, and saw the boat farther out than it had been, but I couldn't see Vinnie. Not good.

Moving past the speed boat, I was shocked to see it upside down on the beach, one engine broken loose and lying in the sand and a gaping hole in its side that had been made by the rocks near the beach.

Duke wasn't kidding!

I scanned for Martinelli's track trail and found it in a few seconds. It headed through the huge stone arch in the direction of the second beach, Graciella's tracks right beside them. She was half walking, half being dragged.

Getting my act together took a few moments. The swim in had left me panting, even though I was in very good shape from trail running with Rosa. I started after Martinelli and Graciella hoping the psycho hadn't kidnapped her just so he could kill her before he made whatever getaway he had planned. That seemed like it might be his style.

Coming through the arch, seagulls squawked above me and as I came back into the sunlight, I saw the second beach was quite a bit bigger than the other, angling up into a large flat as it neared the cliffs. Ahead, I saw them, Martinelli looking out to sea, toward the north and Graciela sitting in the sand, her head in her hands. A huge military duffle sat at Martinelli's feet.

Sneaking toward them, I did my best to stay in the shadow of the huge rock formation I had just emerged from. With a man like Martinelli, the advantage of surprise was not something to be lightly thrown away.

Truth be told, I hadn't realized how much the idea of facing him again scared me, but my hammering heart let me know in no uncertain terms. The impromptu plan had been to double team him, but having no idea where Vinnie was, or if he was even coming, there was a good chance I was going to have to confront the bastard all by my lonesome.

I was less than thirty feet away when Martinelli noticed me.

"Oh, you have GOT to be shitting me!" he growled.

I didn't say a word. I wanted to place myself between Graciella and the bastard who had brought her here. Martinelli reached into the duffle and pulled out a Wal-Mart machete with a curved eighteen-inch blade and an orange plastic handle. He thwarted my plan, moving closer to Graci.

"Oh no, sonny. That ain't happening," he said. "You and yours been so good to me, leadin' me around this island, helpin' me find the man with the money. Got to hand it to you, you're a tenacious punk."

"Gee," I replied, my voice flat, "you're so welcome."

"I probably wouldn't have smoked old man Brender out if it hadn't been for you. The fact that you idiots couldn't seem to figure out I had your phones and messenger app hacked made my life so much easier."

"You didn't need to kill Jordan Brender's lover," I said.

He shrugged. "The whiny little bitch hit me with some cheap-ass pepper spray. I been sprayed more times in training than I care to remember, and it don't stop me. He found that out the hard way. Actually, I really just enjoyed shutting his snarky little mouth permanently."

"Look, man, let Graciella walk away with me, we'll go back to the other beach and whoever's coming for you can just pick you and your ill-gotten gains up. No one else needs to get hurt, and I won't interfere with you anymore."

Graciella looked up at him, fear in her eyes, and I saw he had hit her again. One side of her face was bruised and swollen. Martinelli turned to her, a patronizing smile on his face. Facing me again, he shook his head.

"She's mine. Mine to do with as I please, and nobody takes what's mine," he said. "I'll make you a counter offer. You turn around now, march through the arch to the other beach, outta my airspace, and I'll let you live."

"We're at an impasse then, 'cause I'm not leaving without her."

"Yeah. I kinda figured that, oh gallant hero," he said, lunging at me with a full overhand swing of the machete.

It's unwise to try to block a heavy piece of sharp steel with direct force. I batted the blade away from me with the gaff end of my short staff, hoping to hook his weapon. That didn't work, but I knocked it aside far enough that it threw him off balance and I thrust the other end at him like a pool cue. He danced back out of range, and I inwardly cursed that my staff was only five feet long.

Martinelli was not only ridiculously strong, but he was fast too. My main hope was age. He was in his late thirties, maybe early forties. I was mid-twenties and had been trail running for the last year. If I could draw this out, I might have a conditioning advantage.

It was a pretty big maybe, and I had to stay alive long enough for that to happen.

I swung at the machete, hoping again to hook it out of his hands, and Martinelli spun away 360 degrees. He brought the blade around at the end of his arc and it was only my diving in a forward roll that kept me from getting a permanent haircut.

I came to my feet, knowing he was right behind me and used his own spin tactic to avoid the tremendous chop he'd been aiming at my neck. His momentum carried him by me, and this time I ignored the weapon and went for his leg with the gaff. I caught him about mid-calf, and I could feel the sharp hook slide into his flesh.

"Ahhh! Shit!" he screamed. I tried to yank him off his feet, but he had turned so the gaff came out cleanly. Nonetheless, a dribbling stream of blood trickled down his leg, clumping in the fine volcanic sand.

"First blood to you, boy," he grinned an evil grin. "Last blood to me."

"Talk's cheap," I replied.

"Yep," he said, limping forward and slashing in a figure eight pattern. A less-strong person might have been getting tired by this point, but Martinelli seemed to actually enjoy the pain. I kept trying to swat aside the slashes with the short staff, but every few passes I'd barely get my deflection up in time. The machete was biting chunks out of the staff, and I barely missed losing fingers twice.

"Daniel!" I heard Graciella yell. Out of the corner of my eye, I saw her spinning, holding on to something large, and when the heavy duffle collided with Martinelli I saw what it was. It must have been pretty full of something, because it caught him in the ribs and knocked him off balance.

He turned, literally growling like a rabid dog and advanced on her as fast as his damaged leg would allow.

"Run, Graci! Head for the other beach!" I yelled to her. She saw the situation immediately, that her attacker couldn't keep up, and headed back the way we'd come at a sprint. Martinelli tried using his rage to carry him to her, but the pain in his leg allowed her to get a huge lead quickly. I intercepted him and hit him in the ribs with a hard side kick before he saw me coming. It staggered him a moment, almost taking him off his feet, and I followed with the staff, trying to hook his other leg.

"Not again, you shithead!" he snarled. He knocked the staff aside and caught it dead center with the heavy steel blade. Luck was not with me. It hit a spot already chipped and went right through the wooden dowel. The upside was that I was now holding two weapons, the downside that they were both of shorter reach than the machete.

"Graaaaaa!" Martinelli came at me swinging furiously, and I used both separated ends of the stick to swat away the strikes. I tried to get sideways to his line of attack, but he was coming at me so hard and heavy I had no chance to do anything but defend. If all you can do is defend in an attack like this, eventually something's going to get through.

He swung low, and I blocked with my left stick but couldn't completely absorb the energy from the heavy strike, and I felt the blade bite into my left leg at exactly the same point I had taken an arrow's broadhead two years before. The pain shot up behind my eyes like a lightning bolt.

It's very hard to do anything when you're hit by pain like that, and the only thing that kept me from having that Wal-Mart special buried in my collarbone was the hours spent in the dojo trying to keep my seniors from crushing me. I threw myself back, but not quite fast enough. I felt a terrible burn and pulling sensation across my chest muscles and instantly felt warm liquid running down over my belly.

Martinelli concentrated his attack, swinging the blade high as if to split me in two. With my attention focused on the machete, he slid in and hit me with a heavy left cross, bringing a shower of stars in front of my eyes. I tried to keep my feet, but I went down backwards, trying to do a reverse shoulder roll to my feet. I was half-stunned and lost my balance, went down and I knew it was over. There was no way I'd make it back to my feet before he finished me and even if I did, I was hurt bad enough I doubted I'd be able to defend very well.

I looked up defiantly at Martinelli, determined not to die like a punk, and he smiled a smug smile as he raised the big knife, preparing to send a rain of cuts down on me. As he stepped forward, something round, about the size of a soccer ball slammed into his head and he staggered sideways, dropping the machete. A plastic fishnet float bounced onto the sand and a soaking-wet Vinnie slammed into my opponent like a linebacker.

Vinnie hit him twice in the face, then tried to get a forearm choke on Martinelli, straddling him and using his superior size to hold the man down. As I tried and failed to stand, Martinelli reached up with his gorilla-like arms and cross-grabbed Vinnie's collar to reverse the choke. Vinn was having trouble in just a few seconds. It was a classic Judo choke, designed to cut the flow of oxygen to the brain and Vinnie couldn't break Martinelli's iron grip.

I climbed to my feet, dizzy and sick and hobbled to where the machete lay. I almost passed out picking it up, and as I turned towards the combatants, Vinnie's eyes rolled up in his head and he went limp.

"Martinelli!" I yelled, waving the sword. I wanted him distracted so he couldn't employ his favorite neck-breaking technique on one of my best friends. Fortunately, I got his attention. He stood, blood trickling from a cut over his eyebrow.

"Boy, you're on your last legs, bleeding' out. You can barely stand. I'm gonna take that blade away from you and y'know what I'm gonna do with it? Shove it up your ass. Then I'm gonna come back and stomp on the big boys skull 'til his brains come spurtin' out his ears." He grinned. "And if there's time after that, I'm gonna go collect my bitch. Give her a good beating, too."

"Remember?" I said, "Talk is cheap." I didn't feel a quarter as brave as that sounded.

He nodded and started forward, but stopped as we both heard an unmistakable sound coming in from the ocean. Looking that way, I saw a sleek heavy-duty looking black helicopter with landing gear up skimming the waves, coming in our direction. The craft came over the beach, throwing a truly prodigious amount of sand in the air as they lowered their gear. We were both momentarily blinded, but when the flying sand grew less, I saw Martinelli pick up the duffel.

"Screw this," he said. "Them boys gotta do what I say, but they ain't gonna stay around forever. They got 'plausible deniability' to maintain. I suggest you do the smart thing and don't try to get in my way ever again. The bitch ain't worth it, but what's in this here duffle is my livelihood south of the border for a very long time. I'm takin' it and if you're wise, you won't interfere."

I hated this man, but I could feel my strength draining away with the sand-peppered blood running down my torso. I gestured toward the helicopter with the machete.

"Just… go. And may you get what's coming to you someday. In spades."

He smiled his ugly smile and patted the duffle.

"Already got mine." He started limping to the helicopter.

"Oooh crap…" Vinnie was trying to sit up. I went over to him. "Mac… dude's gettin' away."

"Vinn, we're alive. Graci's alive and not in his grasp. Let's take what win we can," I said. "Besides, he's evidently got some sort of allies in that bird, and from what we know they're probably spook-connected. I don't even want to try at this point."

"Shit, Mac!" Vinnie said. "Bro, you are covered with blood!"

"Nothing deep, looks worse than it is."

"That's not sayin' much, Mac! 'Cause it looks pretty bad from here."

"Vinn," I interrupted. "Look."

Martinelli had almost made it to the chopper when two men in black fatigue uniforms and ball caps got out to meet him. I couldn't hear anything but I saw our enemy start a little swagger to his limping gate as he approached them. His body language was that of someone who held all the cards, and he pointed at the two with what could only be the attributes of someone putting someone else in their place.

The two men looked at each other, then one began shouting to Martinelli. We couldn't hear what was said over the running helicopter engine, but the murderer's entire body language changed.

He pulled the duffle in front of himself, and began to walk slowly backward. The arrogance was gone, and his bearing was that of someone suddenly very afraid.

Both men stepped toward him, and I could faintly hear Martinelli yelling something at them, though I couldn't make it out. He held the duffle out to them as an offering. Both men looked at the duffle, then simultaneously drew handguns and opened up on our now-helpless opponent.

He dropped the bag and tried to run on his wounded leg, but numerous red spots appeared on his back and he went down on all fours. One of his assailants calmly walked up behind him and fired at least four or five shots into the back of Martinelli's head. The result was, to say the least, gruesome.

Both men looked down at him for a moment then grabbed his feet and dragged him, head bouncing, through the sand to the helicopter, leaving a trail of gritty blood. They flopped him inside the back compartment, kicking his legs in when they stuck out.

"That… was brutal," I said.

"Yeah, but Mac? Guess what. We're witnesses."

"Oh… that's not good."

Sure enough, one of the two men was walking our way. The other seemed to be picking up shell casings.

"Vinn, run. Maybe you and Graci can get up the coast, into the water or something," I said, racking my brain as to how we'd get out of this.

"Yeah right," he said. "Like I could ever face Rosa if I did that."

"But…"

"Just shut it dude. That copter has a mini-gun. We're screwed, so let's see how this plays out."

The man, the agent, calmly walked up to us, making no move to pull his weapon. He looked at the two of us, sitting there, beat to hell and nodded.

"Pretty brave," he said. "Going after that bastard."

"You gonna eliminate the witnesses?" Vinnie asked.

He looked out over the ocean for a moment, then back at us. "I hope not. It depends on you."

"You… have… our complete attention," I said.

"That man was blackmailing your government. What branch of that government is not important, other than to know that he was one of ours, learned some compromising things that could not go public and has been using them to leverage money and technical support for several years now. Most of what he wanted wasn't enough to bother shutting him down until the last couple weeks, when he grew very demanding."

"I take it that whatever he had, it's no longer a threat," Vinnie said, trying to be as vague as possible.

"You'd be correct. What he had, we found, and his back-ups and dead-man eventualities were found also. Details are not important. What is important is that he threatened powerful people and the threat has been neutralized."

"Yeah. Most definitely," I said, noting the other agent scooping up Martinelli's sandy blood with a wide shovel.

"Just so." The man allowed himself the shadow of a smile and took in the cliffs behind us. "Which brings us to you two. I am going to give you the story and you will tell the authorities verbatim what I tell you. Do you agree to this?" Vinnie looked over at me, and I nodded. Vinnie nodded, too.

There are times when trying to be Don Quixote will get you eaten by the windmill.

The agent gave us our script, walked back to the helicopter and got in. It raised in a flurry of sand, and I expected that they would fly away with their grizzly prize. The copter instead flew over the arch to the other beach and disappeared. A few minutes later, Graciella came running to us.

"What is going on?" she said. "There are guys in a helicopter hooking some kind of straps to David's boat! And where is that bastard? Oh my God, Mac! You're bleeding!"

"Graciella? Listen to me, I have a story to tell you," Vinnie said as the helicopter flew out over the ocean carrying the speedboat.

CHAPTER TWENTY-SEVEN

***

The two agents had shown no interest in taking the duffle full of Brender's ill-gotten gains with them, and Vinnie took it up into the cliffs and hid it. When the Kauai PD showed up in their launch, we had our script down pat. Martinelli had almost killed us, then escaped in his boat. The blown sand from the helicopter had erased or buried Martinelli's blood and tracks from existence, so the only blood to be found was mine.

Vinnie and Graciella had torn up their own clothes to bind up my cuts. They almost looked like swimwear models if you didn't look too close and saw that they were in their underwear. The bruises they each bore kind of ruined the illusion, anyway.

The police took photos of everything, telling me that tomorrow the wind and the waves would have made the entire beach almost new again. Not the best environment for preserving evidence. They ferried us out to Duke's boat and Rosa almost had an aneurysm when she saw my condition. It was a fast trip to Port Allen and the Lihue hospital.

The ocean was calmer the next day when Vinnie and Duke came out and surreptitiously picked up the duffle. When we counted the cash in it, Brender's cash stash amounted to just about seven thousand dollars more than the total he had scammed from Melinda and my mom. The vote was unanimous that the duffle of money had "gotten away with Martinelli" and was nowhere to be found. Our people were at least going to get their money back.

Three days later, the speedboat rented by one J.T. Wilcox, a.k.a. David Martinelli, was found floating half submerged in the ocean. It was assumed that Wilcox/Martinelli was lost at sea. And maybe he was. How much effort does it take to kick a corpse out of a helicopter?

As for myself, I took thirty-four stitches across my chest and eighteen in my left leg. I lay in the hospital, with a much calmer Rosa at my bedside when my uncle came in and almost had an aneurism of his own.

"Goddam it, Mac!" he started on his tirade, "how could you be so crazy as to chase that gorilla down with no firearms? Vinnie said you took that crazy son of a bitch on with nothing more than a fish gaff. What is wrong with your head? You should have just let him go, and let the police search for his ass. You didn't owe Brender or his dead pal anything, and we have the passwords for Brender's accounts so justice will be served there."

"Uncle Gil," I said, "he had Graciella. He was going to take her somewhere and do horrible things to her, then probably kill her. Vinnie and I were not going to let that happen, and you know damn well if you'd been there you'd have gone after him too. Sometimes you just have to cowboy up and tackle things head-on if you ever want to be able to look at yourself in a mirror again."

"Jesus, when your mother sees you, she's gonna have a fit and fall in it!"

After all this time, I'd had enough.

"Uncle, look right here," I said. "Right in my eyes, and listen. I am twenty-five years old. I am a man. You and my mom can't protect me from the world, but you've both given me the tools to cope with it. I do not ever want to have this conversation again, sir."

He didn't answer.

"I control my own destiny, for better or worse."

He blinked, nodded, and said, “Get healed up fast. We’ve still got work to do, Mister Man.” He turned on his heel and left.

“Damn, I think I just kicked him right in the feels,” I said, watching him walk away.

“He had to hear it,” Rosa said. “Too bad you’re all on the injured reserve, though.”

“Oh?”

“Yep. ‘Cause you have no idea how hot I feel for you right after that little speech.”

“Y’know, I’m not really that badly hurt.”

“Rest now, Tarzan. Tomorrow’s another day.”

CHAPTER TWENTY-EIGHT

***

A month later, Vinnie and I said goodbye to Duke off the coast of Washington State. He and cousin Sonny had chartered a boat large enough for the four of us to journey from Kauai, and the lot of us traveled the entire distance across the Pacific. Vinnie and I became crewmembers in good standing.

We pulled the boat's Zodiac raft up on the beach during high tide at two a.m., then pushed it back out far enough that Duke could return to the boat. We waved goodbye and carried our two backpacks up the shore.

There was no way around it, we were now smugglers.

Nondescript, the company "no one will notice" Acura, was waiting on a road just up from the beach. Next to one of those little solar LED lanterns, my uncle was sitting on a log looking like he wished he hadn't given up smoking several years ago.

"Bout time you two got here," his gravelly voice carried out over the sand to us. "I was about to call it a night and go to Denny's for pie."

"Good to see you too, Uncle."

"Got everything?" he said, gesturing to our packs.

"Yeah, Gil," Vinnie said, "but let's not hang out and admire the fog. The authorities might have some questions if they found us with all this cash, and I really don't feel like 'splainin' it to 'em."

There was no stopping at Denny's. We did manage to hit the McDonald's in North Bend for breakfast coffee and bathroom before we crossed the Cascades into 'Eastern Washington'. A quick fill-up at a gas station and we once again hit I-90 and burned for home.

It's a funny thing what the United States has become. I used to think my uncle was a raving paranoid, but I knew if we were found with this much cash in hand, even if it had been fresh out of our own bank accounts, we'd have a great deal of difficulty with the authorities. In some states, the law might instantly assume we were involved with drug trafficking and confiscate it. There's more than a little evidence to support the theory that our government likes to know where all our money is at any given time, so they can get to it if they feel the need.

The fact was, that if this particular cash was brought to light, it was likely that it might take years of legal wrangling for Melinda and Mom to get it back. That made us very cautious on the drive home. At least two of Brender's victims were going to get most of their money back without waiting for years and having to hire lawyers to keep everyone honest.

***

We waited almost six months, but Chambers and Associates received a fat check from the association of Brender's victims. As we thought, the money from the swindler's accounts was tied up in the courts, but it looked like the victims would get a good portion of their money back. Eventually.

We also had received a bounty from the authorities so probably for the first time in his life, Jordan Brender actually made money for other people, instead of fleecing them out of it. I'm sure the irony was lost on him as he sat in jail awaiting trial, his assets all frozen to the point of being unable to make bail.

Ed, Melinda, Uncle Gil, Rosa, and myself, were sitting in the lawn chairs and tables that my uncle kept on his deck to admire the sunsets here in the flatlands. My mom had also joined us.

"We never saw sunsets like this when we were living in the

rainforest near North Bend," Mom said.

"We were in a forested canyon," I said. "In a place that got ninety inches of rain a year. We ran and hid in terror when the sun came out."

"Oh, we did not," she said, perhaps worried that our friends might take my claim at face value.

"How is your chest doing, Mac?" Melinda asked.

"Eh, I can do pushups again, and I have a bitchin' pirate scar." I rolled up my shorts, "Plus, here on the left thigh I've got a nice crisscross scar. Maybe I should get some tattoos next."

"Maybe you should stop getting in situations where people are giving you scars," Mom said.

"With Mister Trouble Magnet, that could prove difficult," Rosa said.

Hoping Rosa was wrong, we all laughed, all except Melinda.

"You okay, Mel?" Uncle Gil asked. "You seem awfully quiet tonight."

She fidgeted in her chair for a moment, clearly uncomfortable. "I… uh… I think it's time for me to move on."

We were all surprised, and a little dismayed, none moreso than Ed. Melinda had become almost like family in a very short time.

"Why, Mel?" Ed said. "Was it something I said?"

"No, you silly man," Mel replied. "You've been wonderful. It's me. I've been freeloading off Gil here for over eight months. He's done so much for me, you all have, that I just feel sort of like… a parasite."

"Oh no, Mel…" Ed started.

"Mel!" Uncle Gil interrupted. "You paid all our expenses on that trip, right?"

"Yes, but I still came out ahead, and…"

"You've been making me and Ed coffee, baking, helped me straighten out that accounting mess last week, just how are you not pulling your weight?"

"I just feel like I've haven't been."

"Look, you've been a godsend. Me and this old badger just have too much testosterone to be left all alone out here unsupervised. Ed? I think we should formally adopt Mel. Whatcha think?"

"Seconded," Ed said, "and damned happy if she'd stay."

"You two really mean that?"

"As much as Duke did when he asked Graci to come live with him," Uncle Gil told her.

"Hmmmm. As I recall, there was romance involved there."

Slowly and obviously, Uncle Gil turned and looked pointedly at Ed Burnbaum. Ed turned bright red.

"I'd," Ed hesitated, then seemed to find his courage. "If you'd stay, it'd make me the happiest fella on Earth."

Melinda looked at him for a moment, then stood, walked over and put her arms around him.

"Well," she said, "we can't have a bastion of testosterone, can we? I think I will, stay that is. Truth be told, I didn't want to go, but I didn't want to be a burden, either."

The relief on Ed's face was both comical and touching.

"Besides that," Uncle Gil said, "Cat-cat and McGow probably wouldn't sign off on you leaving."

"Oh my. I hadn't even thought about that."

"Well, now, with that settled," I said, "I think Rosa and I need to head out. We've got a big day tomorrow."

"Oh?" Uncle Gil said.

"Sî, Gilbert. Mac and I have been invited to join a trail racing team competing in the Cross Cascade marathon trail run." Rosa told him. "It runs from Snoqualmie Pass to Stevens Pass, almost seventy-five miles on the Pacific Crest trail. We're gonna train with some real pros."

"So… you run through some of the hardest country in the central Cascade Mountains of Washington," Uncle Gil said, "with what I assume will be minimal gear, and you aren't worried at all?"

"Uncle Gil," I said with a slight laugh. "What could possibly go wrong?"

Friends and family. Sometimes they give you the oddest looks.

END

Acknowledgments and afterword

Just a note from Clint...

If you're wondering, yes, some of the things that happen to Mac in my books have happened to me. I've never had to face off with a psycho killer though, let me make that perfectly clear. With the issues of smoke and fire, I and my fellow north central Washingtonians deal with large fires almost every summer nowadays. The chapter with the exploding propane tanks and burning warehouses was based on actual events.

Not all of the episodes are bad. My wife, Suzie makes a cameo in this book. She's the red-head in the shorty wetsuit. When she and I visited Kauai, she took fish food snorkeling with us, stuffing it down into her suit. The frenzied fish feeding is not fiction, but what wasn't in this Mac story is the aftermath of the fish feeding. Suzie hadn't realized that a portion of her fish food had leaked into her wetsuit and was dribbling out the bottom. We had a tough time figuring out why all these large and colorful fish wouldn't leave her alone, no matter where she swam.

I hope you enjoyed the story. Thank you very much for reading it! If you liked it, also note that this is the third of Mac's adventures. The first book in this series is *The Sage Wind Blows Cold*, the second is *Death in the High Lonesome*. Mac earns his reputation as a trouble magnet in those stories, also.

Special thanks to Suzette Hollingsworth, J.S. Brady, Daniela Morescalchi, Ruth Dagraca, John Barta, Brian Greiner, and editors Deb Nemeth, May Peterson and Tina Winograd for helping me beat this thing into a semblance of a professional novel. I made these poor souls work WAY too hard. It takes a small army to pre-read and proofread me.

AFTERWORD

I hope you enjoyed this new adult thriller which draws on my survival/nature training with Tom Brown, Jr., Earthwork Northwest and Jon Young and my black belt karate training in Goju-ryu. There's much more to come in this Mac Crow series! I have a whole world of adventure for Mac and Rosa.

If you'd like to learn more about my books and graphic novels, you can find more about me at my website, **clinthollingsworth.com**. If you'd like to keep up with what I am doing, please sign up for my newsletter. It will have book and comic news, articles on survival and nature, general fun musings and links to cool stuff. You can sign up here.

If you enjoyed *The Deep Blue Crush*, it is most appreciated if you could take the time to post a review. These days, authors seem to live or die by the number of reviews they have. It could mean the difference between going back to my day job or continuing my writing career, so I thank you in advance.

My wife, Suzette Hollingsworth, has written a Sherlock Holmes series, if you are in the market for witty banter, mystery, and romance.

If you'd like to read a post-apocalyptic adventure check out *The Wandering Ones (wanderingones.com)* webcomic. If humor is more your game, try our semi-auto biographical webcomic Starting From Scratch (startingfromscratchcomic.com).

Thanks for reading!
-Clint Hollingsworth

Other NOVELS by Clint Hollingsworth

The Sage Wind Blows Cold

Deep in the woods, desperately following the trail, Mac comes upon an SAR volunteer face down in the forest with an arrow in his back. Little does MacKenzie Crow know, this is just the beginning of his problems.

Death in the High Lonesome

Mac and Rosa must escape from the deep mountains, with minimal gear during a blizzard, and to make things worse, they are being tracked by a killer who always seems to be three steps ahead of them. If Mac's skills of survival and tracking fail them, his and Rosa's bodies won't be found until spring time.

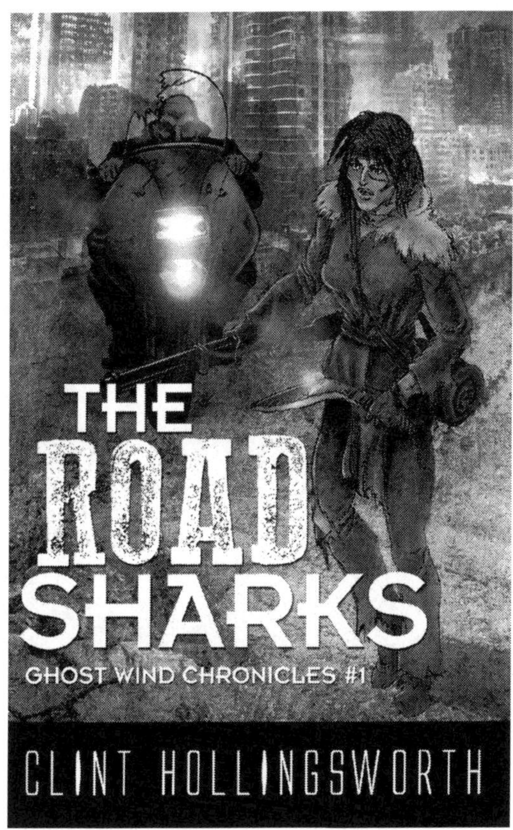

The Road Sharks (Ghost Wind Chronicles #1)

The story of Ravenwing's (The Wandering Ones) banished sister, **Ghost Wind.**

In 2057, warrior scout Ghost Wind finds herself banished from her people, cast adrift in a world ravaged by a man-made bio plague. Looking for a new home, she meets Eli, the handsome rider with many secrets, who hints at a place she might be welcome. Unfortunately, she also meets the vicious fusion cycle gang,the Road Sharks who do their best to make her life a living hell.

To survive, to have a new home, Ghost Wind realizes that she must be just as ruthless as her enemies, and that standing on the sidelines is a good way to lose everything.

Graphic NOVELS by Clint Hollingsworth
Available on Amazon

The Wandering Ones

2066 A.D.-The Pacific Northwest. A man-made plague has wiped ou 80% of the world's population, dividing the survivors into the Clan o the Hawk (following the way of ancient Apache scout warriors, Ninja and Trackers); the Western Alliance, a technology based society; an the Neo-Nazi Farnham's Empire.

It's been thirty years since the great Die-Off. Ravenwing, master scou of the Clan of the Hawk must take in three untrained apprentices fron the technological Western Alliance, and teach them how to survive i the brutal post apocalyptic world of 2066 a.d.

Made in the USA
Middletown, DE
21 January 2025